To Mark.
with Best Wishes
Christmas 1977.
from Geo. Brice.

ROBIN HOOD

See page 157

A man on a black horse . . . turned . . . to ride away

ROBIN HOOD
THE PRINCE OF OUTLAWS
a tale of the fourteenth century
from the 'Lytell Geste'
by
CAROLA OMAN

*Illustrated with line drawings
and 8 colour plates by*
S. VAN ABBÉ, R.B.A., A.R.E.

LONDON: J. M. DENT & SONS LTD.
NEW YORK: E. P. DUTTON & CO. INC.

CAROLA OMAN (Lady Lenanton) was born and brought up at Oxford, where her father was Chichele Professor of Modern History.

She went to Wychwood School when she was seven, and was already writing poems and stories which she illustrated herself, and later wrote historical plays at school. Her first book, a volume of poems, was published in 1921. The following year she married and lived in London. Then she and her husband went to live in Hertfordshire in an old house that was built in the year that Charles I was born.

In London, Carola Oman wrote historical and modern novels; in the country she writes historical biographies and books for children.

She once had three spotted dogs called after the Plantagenet kings—Edward, Richard, and John— and a black Labrador called Prince Rupert.

All rights reserved by J. M. Dent & Sons Ltd, Aldine House, Albemarle Street, London. Made in Great Britain at The Aldine Press, Letchworth, Herts. First published 1939. First published in this edition 1949. Last reprinted 1974

ISBN 0 460 05007 9

CONTENTS

CONTENTS

PART FOUR

ROBIN, MARIAN, AND THE KING

ILLUSTRATIONS

COLOUR

BLACK AND WHITE

PREFACE

ONE day I went up to London in answer to a letter about writing a book for a children's series.

When I was told the subject—'It's Robin Hood'— I looked out of the window at the pale London streets and I thought of green archers stopping jangling processions of fat priests and merchants in the heart of the sun-dappled forest, full of outlaws and deer and foxes and butterflies and birds and squirrels. . . . I thought I should like to write a new Robin Hood, taking the story from the oldest ballads I could find, and describing the food and clothes and sports and daily life, in town and country, of real people who lived in England in Robin Hood's days.

I collected all the books I could find about him, brought them down to the country and began to read them. I soon discovered that although 'Rymes of Robyn Hood' were popular with the English peasantry as long ago as 1377—the year that Richard II came to the throne—to-day most scholars who have studied the facts have decided that Robin Hood cannot be seriously considered as an historical character.

This may easily sound more depressing than it really is. Of course there were outlaw captains who performed some of the deeds attributed to Robin Hood, and one of them may have borne that name or nickname, and been an incomparable sportsman and the friend of all the poor and downtrodden. But the character which has crystallized as one particular hero was probably made up from life-stories of a succession of men living at various dates between the Norman Conquest and the

Wars of the Roses—men who might have made good subjects, but were driven to be outlaws by the oppressive forest laws and the glaring corruption of Church and State. This was especially likely to happen at times when the King was absent from his country, or a child, or a weak man, and it is noticeable that three separate early ballads of Robin Hood are set in such times.

Some people have tried to prove that Robin Hood was really the same character as Robin Goodfellow or Puck, a mythical spirit of the woods. Others have had no doubt that he flourished in the reigns of Richard Cœur de Lion, John, and Henry III. Certainly Randolf, Earl of Chester, with whom his name is coupled at its earliest mention as a ballad hero, really lived then, and Scottish chroniclers of the fifteenth century all assign Robin to about this period.

One of the most ingenious theories is that he was a real 'Robyn Hode,' who is mentioned in contemporary documents as having served in the household of Edward II shortly after that King had made a stay at Nottingham. But other contemporary documents show that Robin Hood was not an uncommon English name then.

Whatever their origin, by the middle of the fourteenth century ballads of Robin Hood were being sung all over England, and by the end of the Wars of the Roses May Day was known as Robin Hood's Festival, and men dressed as him, Little John, and Friar Tuck, performed plays about him, and led processions of mummers and merrymakers. Maypoles and morris dances were soon added to these celebrations, and Robin was given a fair lady— Maid Marian, the Queen of the May—as his companion, and declared to have been of noble birth.

Shakespeare knew all about Robin, and mentions him

in two of his plays. In *As You Like It* he says that the banished duke lives in the forest of Arden with many merry men, 'like the old Robin Hood of England,' and that 'young gentlemen flock to him every day, and fleet the time carelessly, as they did in the golden world.' But even in Shakespeare's time, 'Tales of Robin Hood are good for fools' was a proverbial expression.

Later historians took Robin much more seriously. They published lives of him, and gave him a pedigree dating from William the Conqueror. They said he had really been Robert Fitz-Ooth, Earl of Huntingdon, and that Maid Marian had been Matilda, daughter of Earl Fitzwalter. They waxed very warm in defence of their theories and accused one another of 'peevish, weak, and malevolent objections,' and being 'blockheads of the first water.'

I have read thirty-eight ballads about Robin Hood. The story told in this book is taken from the earliest known printed collection. A copy of it, which is, as far as anybody knows, the only copy in the world, is to be seen in Cambridge University Library. I went there to look at it. It was published about 1495 by an Alsatian called Jan van Wynkyn, an apprentice of William Caxton, who introduced the art of printing into England. About fifty years later, an Englishman called Robert Copland, who also, it is believed, worked for Caxton, published another edition of the same ballad. I have seen a copy of it in the British Museum, and it again is believed to be the only copy in the world. Both Wynkyn's and Copland's books are quite small and thin, not more than six inches square and fifty pages long. Both are printed in heavy black-letter type. But Wynkyn's, although the older, looks best to-day, for Copland has used thinner paper, which has gone ribbed and yellow, and his print, which is blurred, shows through on to the next page. Wynkyn says on his title-page: 'Here begynneth a lytell geste of Robyn Hoode, and his meyne, and of the proude Sheryfe of Notyngham.' Copland calls his 'A mery geste of Robyn Hoode,' and adds to it 'a newe playe for to be played in Maye Games, very plesaunte and full of pastyme.'

I have set my story of Robin Hood in the days of Edward II. But I have not made the characters in it speak exactly as they would have done then, because, even had I tried to do so, nobody nowadays would try to read it. For three centuries after the Conquest there was no standard form of English. Every one spoke and wrote in the dialect of his own district. Books written for people who lived in the south had to be translated for the benefit of the men of the north. 'Middle English,' which is the name given to the varieties spoken then, was the dialectal period of our language. I have tried to point out this, by making the archer from London complain of the way that people in Lancashire spoke.

As well as going to the British Museum and to the Cambridge University Library to see the first printed ballads about Robin Hood, I went up to Nottingham and Yorkshire to see the places mentioned in them. Maps of the country round Nottingham are full of places printed in Gothic type—𝔩𝔦𝔨𝔢 𝔱𝔥𝔞𝔱—which means that they are of historical interest. I found amongst them, Robin Hood's larder, and stables and well, and Friar Tuck's well. There are still subterranean passages and caves in the rock under Nottingham Castle.

1939.   C. O.

THE little bandy-legged archer in a scarlet surcoat, and a shining helmet a size too large for him, skipped forward and shouted: 'What d' ye lack, sir?'

He knew that it was not his business to speak first to a gentleman on horseback, unless the gentleman had crooked a finger at him, to beckon him out of the crowd; and even then he ought to have saluted and stood stiff before he opened his mouth. But he was one of the castle garrison, a Londoner born and bred, and he thought nothing of the slow-witted, slow-speaking folk of his lord's north country.

'Y!' as he was wont to cry, in a dismal yell that was his ordinary speaking voice, 'even the gentry up 'ere talks so broad, a man 'as 'is work cut out gettin' the 'ang of wot they're tryin' to sye!'

He had come down from the castle to watch the animals being driven into the town for the beast fair. There had been plenty to see, for the season was almost Martinmas, when stock that could not be fed and housed throughout the winter was sold to be slain and salted down. But rain had fallen heavily all morning, giving the wind-swept Yorkshire town, overshadowed by its frowning, grape-dark castle, a sombre look, and both the cattle and the marketing women had been, to his mind, a poor show. 'Not a single plump wench with a wink or a giggle in her,' he thought, 'and likewise many a fleece here less than two ounces weight.' He had withdrawn under the shelter given by the overhanging first floor of a house in the Gillygate, and was whistling as he pared his nails with his dagger, when he caught sight of the only horse he had

3

seen to-day at which a wise man would have looked twice down in Smithfield. The fine grey courser had evidently lived hard of late. So had the mild, bewildered-looking gentleman seated droopingly on its back. Dinner-hour in Pomfret had come, and every one else was pressing up towards the castle, against whose walls leant the best taverns in the town. The little bandy-legged archer put away his dagger, skipped forward, and shouted: 'What d' ye lack, sir?'

He stopped, however, out of arm's length, for mild as this gentleman might appear, he was tall and big boned, and the archer had discovered ere now, to his cost, that it was often the custom of people up here to knock down a southerner first, and speak with him afterwards. He had no mind to be caught a buffet for impertinence, on a morning when the cobbles were so miry. Also, as he came closer, and noticed that this rider bore a worn, gilded spur on his heel, and at his side a small faded shield, he added a word to his greeting. 'What d' ye lack, sir knight?'

The knight looked down wonderingly, with mournful grey eyes, and met the glittering gaze of a little London cock-sparrow, with a pale face of sharp features, peering up at him from beneath an over-large helmet. The archer had been served with head-gear of the new pointed type, but his chain mail, half hidden by his flapping scarlet surcoat, was as old and twisted as his limbs. Some relic of the Scots wars. . . . Still, he was as smart as spit and polish could make him, and seemed eager to be helpful. The knight answered in distant, courteous tones: 'Good fellow, I am seeking the Southgate for the Blyth road. But here, I am told, I have come but to the Gillygate.'

'That's right, sir, sir knight,' cried the little man, skipping quite close now. 'This is Gillygate, but Southgate's just around the corner.' He laid a knowledgeable hand on the grey gelding's bridle. 'Let me go before you, sir. I was an 'Obbilour once, and knows a good 'orse w'en I sees one. The Blyth road, you says! A fair sound, and you can't miss it. 'Alf a league outside Southgate you'll find a fork. Don't take the right 'and. That'll lead you to Purston Jaglin. What you wants is the hancient Roman road.' Suddenly he stopped. 'Excuse me, sir, but did you know that you're like to lose a stirrup? There's a good lorimer in Featherstone Lane.'

'I know,' said the knight, 'but I must . . . I will . . . be my own lorimer to-night, in Blyth or Doncaster.'

'That metal,' said the little man, 'won't last so long. Much better 'alt 'ere and 'ave it put to rights, sir knight. Then w'ile you're waitin' you could send up to the castle, tellin' them you're taking the Blyth road.'

'Send up to the castle!' repeated the knight vaguely.

'For an escort, sir, if you're travellin' single over Barnesdale,' explained the archer. The crowd had thinned during the last few moments, and there was nobody within earshot. Yet he added in a voice as near a whisper as he could make it: 'We've been furnishin' escorts recently for good reason.'

For a moment there was silence, broken only by the sound of bubbling gutters. The rain had ceased, and a straggle of sunshine was beginning to break from beneath the heavy clouds, finding high lights in the archer's helmet and on the wet timbers of the upper house-fronts. Presently the knight said, smiling a slow and sad smile: 'I see. I thank you for your warning. Nevertheless I must go on now, and alone.' He noticed that the archer's quick eyes had found a small leather casket fastened to his saddle. 'You see, good fellow,' he said, shaking his head, 'I have no reason to fear any I may meet on my road.'

The little archer understood and stepped back briskly. 'I am sorry, sir. By your leave, though, if you're travellin' so light, as one might say, you wouldn't be thinkin' of *partin'*, so to speak, with this 'orse. It just 'appens I do know a gentleman—from the south—was arskin' me only yesterday if I knew of a fleet courser. Grey was the colour he fancied, too. And if you was thinkin' of a long journey, you'll pardon my suggesting that somethin' sturdier than this lot might serve you better.' He ran a bargainer's eye over the gelding's lean quarters.

The knight answered, gathering his reins: 'Good fellow, this horse will be for sale soon, I fear, but the day is not to-day.'

Unabashed, the archer persisted. 'Well sir, there's some as will take warnings and there's some as will not, but mark my words, you're much mistaken if you think that w'ile you're ridin' that 'orse you 'ave nothin' to fear in Barnesdale.' In a quick, contemptuous voice he spat out: ''E'll 'ave 'im off you.'

'What do you mean?' asked the knight, frowning.

The little man began to rant.

''E's a terror. 'E's 'aunted my life for three seasons. Last midsummer year, w'en I was in the royal garrison at Nottingham Castle, 'e 'ad me out of my bed after curfew no less than nine times. Sherwood was 'is lordship's pleasurin' ground then. Lock and bar Nottingham city as much as you like, 'e comes into it from 'is forest w'enever 'e pleases. Came in one day disguised as a butcher, and sold all 'is meat so cheap that 'is stall was

empty by dinner-time. W'en I moves up 'ere and takes
service with the Earl of Lancaster, I thinks: Peace at last!
But as I looks out from the battlements of yonder castle,
two days after I arrives, wot do I see but a figure seated
most uncomfortable, back to front, in the saddle of a
sharp-trottin' piebald. 'As the piebald's tail in 'is 'ands
for bridle, and is strapped on fast so that no 'arm can
befall 'is 'oliness. The sacristan of Kirklees, no less,
and the lighter by an 'undred pounds than w'en 'e took
the road to Blyth Priory. I said but one word when I
saw that sight.' The archer paused, for greater effect.
''*OOD!*' he announced, staring at the knight. ''Ood's
work.'

The knight stared back at him.

'My castle is in Uttersdale. Of whom do you speak?'

'Bless my soul, sir,' gasped the little archer. ''Aven't
they ever 'eard in Huttersdale of Robin 'Ood?'

Four miles south of Pomfret town, the old Roman road
crossed the River Went for the second time, and began
to climb into dumb, dark country. The gale that had
driven the rain away was blowing great clouds, the
colour of a week-old bruise, across wide skies as yellow
as a lighted horn-lantern. They sailed high above the
knight's bowed head, like noble ships at sea, and the wind
began to pipe in his ears sharp as a boatswain's whistle.

It was an outlaw's wind, and outlaw's weather. The
Went, in flood, swirled into bubbles around the strong
central arch of its low stone bridge, and fled eastwards,
reflecting flashing strands of violet and gold as bright as
those in a herald's coat. There were no villages on this
stretch of road, and few travellers to-day. A couple of
miles past he had caught sight of a hamlet on a little hill,
and a jangling group of farming folk, with empty panniers,

had passed him at a sharp trot and turned away towards it. He had noticed that they had done their marketing early, that they rode silently with set faces, that there were a dozen of them, and that they kept together.

Now, although the road ran dead straight as far as eye could see, he could not detect a single human form upon it. Far away, against the eastern skyline, on a mound above the river, rose a group of wildly tossing firs between whose branches he thought he could make out the square outline of a stone keep. But the undrained moorland that lay between it and the highway was impassable. He plucked his hood of darned knitted stuff closer across his brows, and urged his tired horse up and on. Half a mile later, when he came to a cross-roads, he drew rein, and while the wind wrapped the long tail of his hood around his throat or blew it out, straight as a pennon on a top-mast, he rose in his stirrups to take a better view.

It was then that what the archer in Pomfret had foretold came to pass. The knight lurched sideways, and only saved himself by catching at the painted wooden bow of his saddle. He kicked his right foot free, and his near stirrup clattered to the ground. For a moment he stared at it, as if in sorrowful disbelief. Then dismounting, he picked it up, dried it with a tattered rag which he fetched from his sleeve, and stowed it away in the thin wallet at his waist. The stirrup leather too had broken, and he had ado to make his horse stand while he vaulted into the high saddle again. Up here the gale was roaring like a lion, and made him stagger, even when afoot. He caught the tail of his hood, which was blinding his eyes, and buttoned it inside his bosom. Then, after a last hopeless look at the wide highway, climbing south over brown moorland and line upon line of shadowy trees, he turned downhill towards the brighter west. This denter road, as such deep-threaded lanes were called, might lead to a village where he could find, if not a lorimer, at least a smith and a tanner.

An hour later he was painfully climbing back on to the Roman road, about a quarter of a mile below the place at which he had left it. The denter way had grown narrower and narrower, and so thickly overgrown by gorse and long grass, that he could scarcely tell in which direction it was meant to turn. Acorns from overhanging oak-trees had startled him, pattering down upon his head, and once he had been forced to dismount and free a rearing steed caught across the chest by a long strand of sharp-thorned bramble. Under the mire of the steep downhill track lay slippery boulders and gnarled tree-roots. It had ended at last in a footpath across a sedgy field, beyond which some farm or mill might lie, at the water's edge. He had called out to a swineherd, whom he had seen driving a sow and her litter up from a brackish pond. But at the mere sound of a voice the man had taken to his heels.

On the Roman road the undergrowth was cut back, according to the order of the late King, two hundred yards on either side, for the protection of honest travellers from lurking bandits. The knight was well able, therefore, as he came up the last rise towards it, to see the figures of three men in hunting dress, one of whom seemed to be of more than mortal size. They were lounging against a tall tree on the fringe of the forest, and each man was looking out as if he were waiting for someone. As the knight came closer, the one who was looking his way, shading his eyes from the westering sun, raised an arm and cheered. A pang, as sharp as a lance thrust, as swift as breath passing across a steel mirror, shot through the knight's breast.   But there were three of them, and he had but one stirrup.   He did not even lay his hand to his sword, as they came running down towards him.

A moment later they had encircled him, with linked hands, like children playing ring o' roses.   They sang some uncouth catch as they danced, and their speech was of Yorkshire.   When they had danced their fill, the giant amongst them shook himself free of his fellows, and dropping on one knee, put off his hood, and cried out in a great voice: 'Welcome to the greenwood, gentle knight.   My master has waited for you, fasting, these three hours past.'

'Who is your master?' asked the knight faintly, and the cheerful giant answered: 'Forsooth, Robin Hood!'

The greenwood was not green at this season.   The swishing wet bracken through which the three outlaws brought their captive to their master was warm-hued as a squirrel's fur, and the knight noticed that the leaves which drifted down upon the shoulders of his escort matched their livery.   The winter dress of Robin Hood's men was russet.   Like the deer of their forests, they wore a sober coat throughout the cold months.

There were no grassy rides in this corner of Barnesdale, so the little procession had to pass into the heart of the forest in single file.   The courteous giant who led the way in silence, had the solemn velvety eyes of a bullock, and a curling black beard.   A comical-looking youth, with flopping flaxen hair, a peasant's dish-face, and a fixed grin, walked with a hand on the crupper of the grey gelding's saddle.   Last trod an upstanding raw-boned fellow, with so stout an arm and so frank a look, that any Yorkshire baron might have been glad to call him squire.

The sky visible through the further tree boles was growing scarlet for sunset, so until he heard the crackle of faggots, and smelt wood-smoke and baked meats, the knight did not realize that he was drawing towards a clearing where a blazing fire was being tended by many deer-footed, russet-clad archers. He could not forbear an exclamation of surprise when he came in full sight of Robin Hood's secret home.

The outlaws had felled all the timber for a radius of forty yards, and with it built their captain a forest lodge, as handsome as and larger than several used by the King in his southern chases. The lodge was made of tree-trunks just cut in two and left with the bark still on them, so, like the dress of the outlaws, it faded into the surrounding landscape. It was L-shaped, and had a weather-beaten outer staircase at either end, leading to an upper storey, round which ran a gallery. In front of it, under the shelter of the gallery, waited a trestle table, as long and wide as many in a castle Great Hall, and laid ready for a feast with platters and goblets, some of yellow and white metal.

A double ditch, spanned by two drawbridges, gave access to the clearing, half of which was filled by hides slung on poles. In the glades beyond were tents of hide, each guarded by a shadowy form drooping on a spear.

The knight said softly as they came to a standstill: 'Your captain lives like a prince!'

'He is the prince of outlaws,' answered the bearded giant simply.

'And he has no fear of attack in this pleasaunce?'

The man behind said in a deep, growling voice: 'Let them thaat cooms here to attack haave fear!'

The big man had raised a polished ox-horn set in silver,

and a single beautiful note sounded in the stillness of
autumn Barnesdale. At once, as if by magic, the secret
place became alive with hastening russet-clad figures.
Some crawled out from under the hide screens, others
stepped noiselessly from behind tree-trunks, or slid down
from branches of some of the great oaks overlooking the
scene. A string of hunters, bearing with them the body of
a sleek yeld hind, slung on spears, came trotting over the
drawbridge, accompanied by hounds of every size and
kind. Such men as could not crowd on to the bridges
leapt the double ditch with stag-like bounds, flinging up
their arms and cheering as they jumped. When he found
himself surrounded by seven score of the liveliest-looking
fellows he had ever seen, and found the mired paws of a
couple of greyhounds and a pied talbot caressing his boots,
the knight said in the firmest tones he had used yet:
'Advise me which is your captain, good outlaws.'

'Even now at his lodge door,' said the comical-looking
youth, whom every one called 'Much,' perhaps a joke on
his size. The knight turned in his saddle and saw the
prince of outlaws in the entrance of his lodge, holding
back its curtain of beasts' pelts and smiling at him.

Everything about Robin Hood, thought the weary and
alarmed knight, spoke of the forest in which he lived.
His leaf-brown tunic and long knit-hose were no finer
than those worn by all his followers, but no one would
have mistaken him for less than the captain of his band,
although he was younger than most he commanded. He
was a lean, bronze man from top to toe, and when he
slipped off the leathern hunting-coif which hid his brows,
and dropped to the knee in courteous greeting, the head
which he bowed was covered with curls, as tight as those
on the Golden Fleece, but red as dust. He looked up,

and eyes glossy as a newly fallen chestnut danced with merriment or mockery as he said softly: 'Welcome, sir knight! Welcome indeed, for we have waited for you, fasting, these three hours past!'

The knight raised a stiff arm and answered: 'God save you, good Robin and all your fair men.' The fat youth was urging him to dismount. 'I thought,' murmured the knight uncertainly, 'to have dined this day in Blyth or Doncaster.' But he found himself on his feet, and as he watched his horse led away into some hidden fastness, he felt a grip on his upper arm, lighter, he thought, than that of a mortal man, but also faster. 'You must dine with me,' said smiling Robin Hood, and clapped his hands as a signal.

Out of the lodge came three men. The first bore a silver ewer, the second a basin to match, and folded neatly over the arm of the third were cloths of napery fine enough for a lady's chamber. The outlaw and the knight washed and wiped in silence, then Robin Hood led his guest to the board and placed him on his right hand. With politeness that could not have been excelled in a court, he presented several of his foremost followers to the stranger, but made no attempt to discover a name which his guest did not offer. Well, thought the knight, most of those introduced to him went by nicknames. The black-bearded giant was 'Little John,' the striding dalesman who looked as if he should have been some proud baron's squire, was 'Will Scarlet.' A thin, innocent-faced stripling was 'Gilbert of the White Hand.'

The party that had been cooking over the fire in the centre of the camp began to stagger up, bearing smoking dishes, and again the knight's tired eyes widened in surprise. The outlaw's fare was as rich as everything

else here. For fish they had barrelled sturgeon and
dishes of oysters, and lampreys cooked in honey, besides
fresh sole and turbot. . . . For meat they had beef and
mutton and lamb, roast swan and pheasant, capon and
pigeon-pie, and a savoury stew of numbles of deer. The
bread served was all cocket, the best white bread, and
sweet-smelling hippocras, red clarry, and golden Gascon
wine were set upon the table in flagons.

The outlaws swung their legs under the long board, but
still looked to their master for a sign before they fell to.

'Do gladly, sir knight,' said Robin, and handed him
a tall goblet, silver-gilt set with blear-eyed pearls and
stones of many colours, bright as an abbey window.
It was loot from some abbey, guessed the knight, and
hesitated to lift it to his lips.

'You are right,' said smiling Robin, and clapped his
hands again. 'Fetch us our chaplain, Gilbert, for this
guest knows good men do not feast without a blessing.'

Some renegade monk that has broken cloister after
doing murder or worse, thought the knight, and crossed
himself in horror. But the extraordinary figure who
came scrambling out on all fours from one of the distant
tents wore the habit of a Franciscan Friar, correct in
every detail, except that he had tucked his long skirts
knee-high into a scarlet girdle that matched an enormous
pair of red-stockinged legs. Robin Hood's chaplain had
a face round as the moon and rosy as a child's, twinkling
little pig's eyes, and a tonsure of fuzzy red hair that swore
with his belt and hose. He did not look in the least like
a conscience-stricken murderer as he came hallooing over
the ditches, brandishing an oaken cudgel. All the hounds
in the place ran to meet him, wagging their tails and
barking joyfully.

'My chaplain, Friar Tuck, sir knight,' said Robin, rising, and spying a stranger, all the Friar's jollity dropped from him. After blowing out his cheeks, folding his palms, and closing his eyes, he blessed all here, and their fare, as sonorously as any bishop in minster.

'And now let us have a song while we eat,' said Robin Hood.

Gilbert of the White Hand, who had been seated, eyeing a pigeon pie in a loving manner, rose obediently, and amidst cheers from the outlaws, sprang lightly on to the centre of the long table. Although the board was crowded with dishes and fare he upset nothing. He bowed to the company (pirouetting on a toe) and asked them what song they would have; and a boy who had been standing with a fair white cloth folded over his arm, ran to a nearby tree and fetched from it a harp, in a deerskin case. Sir Richard shook his head sadly, but amongst the names called out by his fellows, Gilbert evidently heard one shouted loudest—or else he had intended to sing it in any case. He swept his fingers over the strings of his harp, raising a soft murmur, and whispered, as if he was telling a secret—*Hind Horn*.

Hind Horn was a story about a poor young Scot, who fell in love with his King's daughter, whose name was Jean, and went overseas to make a fortune so that he could marry her. Before they said farewell he gave her a silver wand, with seven live birds upon it—laverocks, or larks— and she gave him a ring set with seven diamonds. She told him that it was a magic ring, and that if ever he noticed that the diamonds were ceasing to sparkle and glitter, like stars on a frosty night, he would know that her love was waning. Every verse of the song ended with a chorus, and the outlaws sang 'with a fal lal lal,' thumping on the board, and on one another's shoulders. One morning, at the end of seven years, Hind Horn had to sail for home in haste, for he woke to find that the stones in Jean's ring were dull as pewter. He arrived at a great feast in the King's hall, disguised in a patched cloak and hood which he had borrowed from a beggar on the sea-shore, and with a grey wig over his yellow hair. The feast had been going on for forty-two days, which sounded magnificent, and the bride was in the act of handing the loving-cup to all the guests, before she mounted her chariot to go with a strange prince to a strange land. When she handed the cup to Hind Horn he drank it dry, and dropped into it the diamond ring. There was a wonderful dramatic moment when Gilbert cried, in a girl's voice:

> 'O got ye this by sea or land?
> Or got ye it off a dead man's hand?'

and then in a triumphant man's voice:

> 'I got it not by sea!   I got it by land,
> And I got it, madame, out of your own hand.'

It was a story with a happy ending, for Jean said that she would rather beg her bread from town to town, with Hind, than go with a prince, in a brown velvet gown, and with gold scales in her hair; and Hind was able to tell her:

> 'Ye need not cast off your gown of brown.
> For I can make you lady of many a town.'

The last notes of the harper's sweet voice died upon the air. He swung his ribboned harp behind his back, and leapt lightly from the centre of the thronged table on which he had been standing, outlined against a darkling

star-pricked sky the colours of a peacock's tail. The
fire on which the feast had been cooked was dying down
with cracking noises. Other cracking noises came from
beneath the boards, where the hounds of the camp were
finishing the bones flung to them. The ruddy glow threw
fierce lights and shadows on seven score faces all turned
towards their master, and all looking more intent than
they had since the moment of their guest's arrival. Robin
Hood cleaned his dagger on a piece of cocket which he
delivered delicately to a slender greyhound that had been
standing trembling with one paw on his knee. He ran
his finger over the edge of the blade, perhaps to make sure
that it was still keen, felt at his belt for its sheath, but on
some second thought did not send it home. Instead he
laid it on the table near his right hand. 'Still he smiles,'
thought the knight, and roused himself to speak first.
He said:

'*Gramerci*, fair sir, for so good a dinner. I have not
dined so well for three weeks past. Now,' he made to
rise, 'I must be wending my way. But if ever I come
again by this country I shall hope to stand your host
as nobly.'

'*Gramerci*, sir knight,' said Robin Hood, gripping him
by the hand, 'but when I offer a dinner, I never am so
greedy, by dear-worth God, as to expect a dinner in
return. Nay,' and his white teeth glistened, 'such never
was my wont. But—ere you wend—bethink you. Is it
—fitting—that a mere yeoman shall—pay—for a knight's
fare ?'

The knight said hoarsely, staring into the darkness of
the forest: 'I have nothing in my coffers that would equal
half the cost of this night's feast.'

'Little John,' said Robin Hood sharply, 'go look!'

The bearded giant went off at the trot towards the place where the knight's horse had been led away, and turning to his guest again, 'You must pardon,' said Robin Hood, 'such uncouthness on our part; but, you see, last week we had a knight here, swore by St. Austin he had not ten shillings in his coffers. We found—how many was it, Tuck?'

'Ten thousand, besides a goodly lady's girdle of gold-smith's work, I thank the saints,' intoned the Friar piously.

'So—tell me truly what you have,' suggested Robin, picking up his dagger and weighing it on his palm.

The knight said miserably, looking Robin straight in the face: 'But ten shillings is what I truly have.'

Robin Hood shot his dagger home into its sheath.

'Sir knight, if you truly have no more than ten shillings, then will I take not a penny from you. And if you desire more, I will lend it to you.'

Little John had returned with the nail-studded leathern coffer from the knight's saddle bow. It was a small coffer and he looked gloomy as he shook it. Nevertheless, before he made to open it, he spread his mantle carefully over the sward beneath, and Little John's mantle was far from small. The outlaws drew near, craning their necks to see the spoil, and the knight, who was fumbling in his pouch, cried distressfully: 'Pray you, do not burst that lock. I will give you the key, when I can find it.'

'Gilbert,' said Robin Hood, without a change of countenance, 'return the knight his key that he may offer it to Little John.' He added in explanation to his guest: 'Gilbert of the White Hand did not sit next you at the table, but mayhap he gave you of some dish, or helped you to wine at some moment.'

See page 10

The three outlaws brought their captive to their master

The startled knight received the key which should have been in his wallet, from light-fingered Gilbert, and passed it to Little John.   The giant undid the casket and poured from it on to his waiting cloak a meagre stream of silver pennies.

'Count them, Gilbert,' commanded Robin, and returned to his seat while Gilbert sorted into ten heaps of twelve, one hundred and twenty coins each bearing on one side the likeness of a king with long curling hair, crowned with a crown *flory*, and on the other a large cross *pattée*, enclosing a dozen pellets encircled by lettering.

When Gilbert had done, Little John marched up to his master and said blankly:

'Sir, the knight is true enow.'

'I feared it from the moment he would not drink unblessed,' nodded Robin.   'Well . . . bring forth some of the best clarry and invite him to drink with me anew.'

The knight came perforce to seat himself at Robin Hood's side again.   A mile away in the forest a hart roared suddenly.   The knight stifled a shiver.   Robin Hood began silkily:

'Your clothing, sir, is somewhat thin for these parts and hours, I fear.   And yet you must, I think, have money enough somewhere.   But perhaps your acres are barren, and you could not muster the fee called for by the King from landowners that do not desire the honour of knighthood.'

The guest covered his brow and sat in silence, and Robin continued with greater urgency: 'Or perhaps you have been—shall we say—a poor manager and let your estates decay, or again, been one of those luckless fellows whose fate is to quarrel with every one.'

The knight stayed dumb as a statue, and Robin's voice concluded:

'Well—if you are neither of these things, then I can only guess that you have thought to make money by lending it at usury, or fie! spent it on naughty loves.'

At that the knight sat upright and cried out:

'By Him who made me, I have done none of these things! And my ancestors have been wise knights and true a century past. And until two seasons ago I myself was of no ill-repute, and might spend four hundred pounds a year.'

Robin Hood said: 'Even so. And in what manner then didst thou lose thy riches?'

The knight answered humbly: 'From folly, I reckon men will say, and from over-fondness.' But his back was lance-stiff as he declared, staring with faded blue eyes into the greater blue night: 'I had one son, Robin Hood, that should have been my heir. I think,' and his voice gathered courage, 'that any man would have been glad to call my son heir. By the time he was twenty winters old there was not his match in the jousting field in our country. I took him to Tickhill that spring— two years agone. You know the jousts there?'

'Tickhill—best in Yorksheer for jousts and walnuts,' growled Will Scarlet, remembering some past glory.

'And what was his prowess there?' asked Robin, as the knight paused.

'It was not there,' said the knight, faltering. 'Would that it had been. Accidents happen at the jousts— every one knows. . . . It was a week after we had returned home—in a meadow by the riverside. He met one of our neighbours. Our bad neighbour. Every one knows that that ford is ours and has been since my grandsire's time.' He beat with his dry hand upon his knee. 'I would have waited his insults, and mayhap gone to law. But I am not young! There were hot words and they fought. My son won. But he left two men on the field—a knight and a squire—dead.' His voice broke, and he turned away, hiding his face in his sleeve.

'I have left more than two dead men on a field and slept none the worse,' recollected Little John dreamily.

'Drink this, sir,' suggested Will Scarlet, filling a cup.

The knight obeyed, with tears running down his face, and all present liked him the better that he had no shame to weep as he told them: 'I have spent my whole fortune on lawyers to save my son's life, and, what is worse, put all my lands and castles in pledge to a certain rich Abbot.'

'To what Abbot and for what sum?' asked Robin Hood.

'Alas! to the Abbot of St. Mary's, near York, for four hundred pounds. And as you know, ten shillings is all I have left in this world.'

'And if you lose your lands?' asked Robin Hood.

'I shall hie me over the salt seas,' said the knight. 'As a poor pilgrim I shall beg my way from door to door seeking'—his last words dropped quietly as falling leaves —'Jerusalem . . . where Christ lived and died. . . . Calvary. . . .'

After a little silence he rose. 'Farewell, friends all. I am sorry that I could not pay.'

Robin Hood laid a finger on his sleeve: 'But where be your other friends, sir knight? I mean your old friends that knew you in the days of your prosperity.'

The knight said without heat: 'Ah! Robin Hood, have you never seen a wolf in the sheepfold—how all the silly flock flees from the hungry beast? Most of the old friends of Sir Richard at the Lee now turn at his name as if it were that of the devil.   Others—the bolder—when they happen upon him face to face, out-stare him.'

A sudden gulp came from the throat of fat Much. Little John, sitting with an arm flung round the shoulders of Will Scarlet, whose hard grey eyes were wet, unlinked himself to blow his nose hard.   Still Robin Hood persisted sternly:

'Have you no kinsman, Sir Richard at the Lee, that would let you borrow from him?'

'By Him that died on the tree,' said Sir Richard, 'I know of no Peter from whom I may borrow to pay Paul.'

'By Him that shaped both sun and moon,' said Robin, 'then neither Peter's nor Paul's name shall avail you here.'

'I never hoped it,' said the knight.   'My only hope is in Our dear Lady, who until this day never failed me. So in Her name I will bid you all farewell.'

But at that name Robin Hood sprang to his feet.

'By dear-worth God, Sir Richard at the Lee, if you had searched England you could not have found a better surety.   In the name of Our Lady I will lightly lend you four hundred pounds.'

A KNIGHT nobly clad in a long furred gown over new
steel armour, and attended by a giant squire, pressed
north on the Roman road as dawn broke. At a certain
spot on the heights beyond Barnesdale, where a denter
way joined the great road, the knight raised his glove to
his basinet in salute, and cried aloud:

'God bless Robin Hood!'

Daylight broadened and found colour in the knight's
gown — rose scarlet, the most expensive dye. The
housings of the fresh bay stallion beneath him were violet
velvet powdered with gold roses, and his squire wore best
green cloth of Douai, and rode a thundering charger,
black as its owner's beard. Behind them followed two
grooms on stout nags, leading sumpter mules. They
had to waken the warder at the Southgate of Pomfret to
let them into the sleeping town, and his fellow at the
Bondgate to let them forth. When the second man
shouted to ask on whose business they rode thus early,
the squire answered:

'My Lord Abbot's, of St. Mary's, York.'

They crossed the Aire at Knottingley, in full sunlight,
and came in sight of Selby Abbey before noon. Here
the knight would have stayed an hour to rest and feed
their beasts. The squire said:

'Into one abbey we must adventure this day, Sir
Richard. Let that suffice. And did I not hear you
telling my master that this is the very day appointed by
the Abbot for you to redeem your lands?'

'Little John,' said Sir Richard, 'you speak sense.
Only I would not tire borrowed steeds that carry heavy bags.

And I do not think that the Abbot can do business with us to-day, because I have remembered that it is Sunday.'

The squire laughed in his beard.

'Robin Hood's steeds do not tire easily. Let us see York and this Abbot before we remember it is Sunday.'

The Fishergate

So they pressed north, and saw the waters of the Ouse, lying in silver links in meadows to their west, and presently, against a sky the colour of periwinkle flowers, a walled city, containing a royal castle, a great minster, two dozen or so parish churches, and several abbeys and priories, all shining white as sugar in the thin autumn sunshine. The knight pointed, and said:

'Yonder furthest tower, outside the walls, is St. Mary's, and under it prays my Lord Abbot that Sir Richard at the Lee may not come before moonrise this day.'

They entered York by the Fishergate, in the hush that falls upon a town on Sunday after dinner, and went to an inn near the castle. A bush hung out over its doors, in token that the best wine was sold here. At the sound of their horses' hooves coming up the narrow street, a knave ran forth crying that all dinner here was eaten an hour past. When he saw these guests, however, he fled

like a coney into a burrow, and in his stead came forth
the host, his master, bowing and saying that if the gentle
knight would have patience a very short while, he and
his servants should be served a fair dinner.

'Now we are in York City, Little John, give me leave
to remember that it is Sunday,' said the good knight.
And before he would eat, he took his squire into the
nearest church. This happened to be St. Samson's, and
a small girl in the congregation began to screech when
she saw Little John, because she had been well instructed
in the Scriptures, and knew that so large a man must be
the very saint to whom this church belonged, come to
pull down its pillars with his great arms, and squash her flat.

When Sir Richard at the Lee and Little John had
heard Mass and returned thanks to God for bringing
them safe to York, they went back to the tavern and fed.
Then Sir Richard ordered a knave to lead him to an
upper chamber. Here, to Little John's disappointment,
the knight put off the fine gown and arms given him by
Robin Hood, and put on again the old thin tunic and
darned hood in which he had been captured on Barnesdale. He made wild his hair and beard, and said:

'How do I look now?'

'By your pleasure, sir knight,' said Little John, 'you
look very ill-favoured indeed.'

'Such is my pleasure,' said Sir Richard. 'And if
you would forward my design, you too would muster a
humbler look.'

They resaddled their horses and mules, over which
the grooms had been keeping guard, and rode out of
the town by the Bootham Bar, a dark and frowning gate,
decorated by the heads of several Scots raiders who had
tried to take the town by surprise a couple of years past.

St. Mary's Abbey was the richest in Yorkshire, and it occupied a very fine site. Its Close, of fifteen acres, ran down to the ramparts and ditch of the city walls on the south, and to the wide, smiling river on the west.

Bootham Bar, York

It was stoutly walled with grey stone on its other two sides, and in the middle of its north wall was its chief entrance, to Marygate.

Little John lighted down from his black charger and banged on the Marygate, and the porter peeped out of a little iron-barred window, and recognized Sir Richard. His eyes nearly popped out of his head. But he hastened to fling the gates open, and when he saw the bay stallion and the black charger on which the poor knight and his

companion rode, he said in an oily voice that these were
the best horses that he had seen to-day, although he had
spent his whole morning admitting company. 'Some
lofty folk have come to dine with my lord this day, Sir
Richard, and all for love of you, I believe.'

He wanted to conduct their horses and mules to the
stables, to ease them, he said. Sir Richard said 'Not
so,' and after a long look at Little John the porter did
not press his suggestion.

So Little John and Sir Richard, followed by the grooms,
rode past the west door of the Abbey Church, and Sir
Richard uncovered for reverence of the carven saints
upon it. Further on they came to that side of the cloister
over which lay the dormitory. A monk was shaking
some bedding out of one of the dormitory windows, and
Little John muttered: 'Phew! Give me the greenwood.'
At last they came to the great door of the Refectory in
which my Lord Abbot of St. Mary's was sitting at meat
with his monks and guests. They dismounted, and Sir
Richard left Little John and the grooms outside with
the steeds and money-bags, and entered alone, and
dropped on his knee.

The Refectory of St. Mary's Abbey was eighty-two
feet long and thirty-seven feet wide, built of fair grey
stone, and lit by windows of stained glass telling the
story of the Creation. But its windows were set so high
in its walls that half a dozen tall fellows standing on one
another's shoulders could not have looked in at them.
Since the short autumn day was now almost over, they
appeared dark and shiny as a beetle's wings, and showed
nothing but reflections of the torches in the gallery. The
ceiling above them was filled with heavy oak beams, and

the walls below them were hung with tapestries. The floor
was not strewn with rushes, as many floors in halls smaller
than this often were. It was finely paved with square tiles
patterned in yellow and brick-red. When Sir Richard
knelt on them, his knee hid a lily surmounted by a crown.

The Lord Abbot of St. Mary's sat at his well-polished
long table of oak-tree, in a carven chair with arms, comfortably cushioned. On his right hand sat his chief guest,
the High Justice of England, whose face Sir Richard had
reason to know all too well. The High Justice was a
little shrivelled-up man with a parchment-yellow skin,
restless greenish eyes, and a thin grey beard which gave
him a Jew's look. Down in London, years ago, one of
the King's foreign favourites, who had a witty habit of
fitting nicknames to his master's advisers, had called the
High Justice 'Lazarus the Lizard.' Some of the English
nobility had cut off the head of this foreign favourite long
since, but the name given by King Edward's poor Perrot
to the High Justice was still remembered, and every
season grew more apt. This evening he was clothed in
an over-robe of black camlet, hooded, lined and trimmed
with red fox pelts, and under that a gown of yellow velvet,
patterned with black branches. On his head he wore
a white lawn coif, which fastened under his chin, and
by the side of his platter lay his white doe-skin gloves,
sewn with a scarlet thread. He was eating sugared cherries
out of a silver box, and looked remarkably happy, because
he had feared that he might have the Prior on his other side
at meat to-day. But he had found himself placed between
the Abbot and the Sheriff, both of whom he liked.

The Sheriff was one of those old friends that had
pretended not to know Sir Richard when he had met him
in the streets of York town last week. He was a whey-

faced man with long, lank limbs and straw-coloured hair
which he wore brushed straight back from his brow.
He had dozens of little gilt buttons down the front of his
furred tunic and up the seams of his long tight sleeves,
and he kept on his knee a felt hat turned up with pea-
green satin and trimmed with an upstanding tuft of
peacock's tail-feathers.

The Abbot, too, had a mantle lined and trimmed with
furs, to keep him warm, although this was a luxury
forbidden to him by the laws of his order.   His wide
sleeves and hood were well filled with grey squirrel skins,
and he was a large red-faced man, with angry light eyes,
and a quite bald head.   It was cold in the Refectory this
November evening, in spite of a fine fire roaring up the
great chimney at its further end.   By the light of a bunch of
torches stuck into an iron bracket on the wall behind him, a
man might see steam rising from the freshly stewed stuffed
quails which my Lord Abbot was popping in his mouth.

On his left hand sat the Prior, the person next in im-
portance to himself at St. Mary's Abbey, and much hated
by him.   For this Prior was a holy and vigorous man.
His face was thin and noble, like that of a saint, and he
wore no furs, although his long nose with a hump in it
always looked chilly, and his voice and his fingers were
certainly icy, as many of the novices knew.

St. Mary's was a Benedictine abbey, so all the monks
wore black habits.   Black monks with pale faces and
rosy faces, fat and thin, tall and short, young and old,
with tonsures of yellow and black and brown and reddish
hair, sat up and down the long shiny Refectory table this
November evening.   Here and there at its further end
were others of the great guests mentioned by the porter
to Sir Richard, knights of this countryside, attended by

their squires and pages. Dinner should have been over an hour past, but the Abbot liked to sit a space after his meals and gossip. Also he was eating still, although every one else had finished.

As the knight slipped into the hall, the Prior was disagreeing with the Abbot, as usual. He said in his east-wind voice:

'The day is not yet done.'

'It will be very soon though,' said the Sheriff, with the high giggle for which he was famous in York City.

'And then,' remarked the High Cellarer, who like his Abbot had three chins, 'we shall have four hundred pounds a year to spend in this place.' And he rubbed his hands together, perhaps because like many fat men he felt the cold bitterly.

'I should like to propose for the last time,' said the Prior to the Abbot, 'that we do not assume this debtor's property at once, but lend him another hundred pounds for another year.'

The Abbot shut his mouth on a stuffed quail with a snap. He presently said, searching with his fingers in the dish before him for the last left there: 'No! This day twelvemonth he borrowed from us, and the bond was that if he did not repay us to-day we should have his lands and castles.'

'But there may be some good reason that we do not know, for his failure to come here to-day,' suggested the Prior. 'He may be overseas, trying to raise the money from foreign merchants. He may be suffering or sick. . . . How should we feel if we seized lands that have been in his family a hundred winters, and he returned a fortnight after we had taken charge of them, telling a true tale of illness or shipwreck?'

The Prior had raised a preacher's voice, and several of his audience looked up at his fine face as if for guidance. A young squire, offering his master rose-water to dip his fingers after the meal, quite forgot himself. He said suddenly 'I agree!' whereat several souls made assenting noises in their throats. The Abbot heard and lost his temper.

'By God and St. Richard,' he shouted rudely, shaking his fist in the Prior's face, 'thou art ever in my beard!'

'The Knight of the Lee is certainly dead or hung,' reflected the Cellarer comfortingly.

'Indeed,' smiled the Chief Justice, fingering his thin beard, 'I think he will not come now.'

At that Sir Richard opened his lips, and still kneeling at the door, called out: 'Do gladly, Sir Abbot! I am come to hold my day.'

Every one jumped as if one of the figures in the tapestry had spoken. Sir Richard arose, and walking up the length of the hall, dropped on his knee again. There was the width of the Refectory table between him and the Abbot, but all the monks seated opposite their superior slewed round in their seats to see the stranger, so there was no hindrance between Sir Richard and the Abbot's blessing. The Abbot did not bless his waiting guest. He leant across the table and his first words were:

'Hast thou brought me thy pay?'

'Alack!' murmured Sir Richard, with drooping head, 'I have not been able . . .'

'Ha! Thou art a shrewd debtor,' began the Abbot in a roar. But could scarcely keep up the pretence of being anything but delighted. He drew back into his cushions, and raising his golden goblet, said: 'Sir Justice, drink to me.'

The lizard-like Justice raised his cup in return. But he only sipped, for he was too much interested to drink yet. The Abbot, returning to Sir Richard, asked:

'If thou hast not brought thy pay, what dost thou here?'

'I came,' said Sir Richard humbly, 'to ask you to grant me a little longer time.'

The Justice set down his cup and said: 'Impossible! This is the day mentioned in the bond. Unless you have brought the money, you have lost your lands. The law is clear.'

Sir Richard looked up at him, and said: 'Good Sir Justice—I know that you know the law well. But you know me well, too. Stand my friend now, in my need. Speak for my part to my Lord Abbot.'

The Justice buried his nose again in his cup, and muttered disagreeably: 'No, no. I cannot speak for you. I am bound by robe and fee to advise my Lord Abbot here.'

He muttered, but could not meet Sir Richard's eyes, because he knew that he was disobeying the King's statutes in accepting robes and fees from the Abbot in exchange for legal counsel. His duty was to accept such payment from no man but his King.

Sir Richard looked from the Justice to his neighbour, and said: 'Now, good Sir Sheriff, be my friend!'

'Nay, nay. Not I,' said the Sheriff.

'Good Sir Abbot,' said Sir Richard, turning back to him desperately, 'be gentle with me. Have the courtesy to hold my lands and castles for me until I can pay you my debt. I swear to be a good tenant and serve you truly, until I have saved the four hundred pounds I owe you.'

'By Him that died on the tree,' said the Abbot, bringing his fist down with a bang that made the flagons start, 'you shall never get your lands back from me.'

'I must say God-speed then,' said Sir Richard, and added: 'It is well for a man to know before he has need of them who are his true friends.'

The Abbot gave him a loathly look, and sprawled forwards over the table, shouting: 'Out!   False knight!   Out of my hall!'

'Thou liest!' returned Sir Richard. 'By God that made us all, I never was a false knight to you or any man.' He rose stiffly and said: 'And you lack courtesy to suffer a knight to kneel before you so long.'

Before the Abbot could roar again, the Justice, into whose lizard eyes had crept a calculating look, laid a finger on his host's sleeve, and said:

'My lord.   Although certainly the law would be upon your side if you seized this knight's lands and castles, I cannot promise you that you would hold them in peace. Sir Richard has been, I believe, well loved in his country-side.   What further sum would you be prepared to give him in return for his disavowal of any claims to his property?'

The Abbot, after considering the Justice's countenance closely, brought out with an effort: 'If thou advise—a hundred pounds.'

'Give him two,' counselled the Justice.

Sir Richard's voice broke in upon their haggling: 'Nay!   By dear-worth God, you get not my lands so. Though you would offer me a thousand pounds, I never would part with them.   Neither Abbot, Justice, nor Sheriff shall be my heir.'

He raised his hunting-horn to his lips, and blew a single soft blast that echoed in the blue-shadowed beams of the great hall.

Into the Refectory of St. Mary's Abbey marched a

giant squire and a sturdy groom, each carrying in his arms
a ponderous leather bag.　They dumped their loads on
to the Refectory table, and strode back without a word
to fetch another couple of sacks, passed towards them
by an unseen comrade in the darkness without.　Sir
Richard at the Lee cut the thongs of one of the bags with
his dagger, and tipped it on to its side.　Out of its mouth,
on to the polished oak-tree set with the remnants of my
Lord Abbot's good dinner, silver pennies began to tinkle
and tumble.

'Have here thy four hundred pounds, which thou
lentest me, my Lord Abbot,' said Sir Richard's scornful
voice.　'If thou hadst been courteous at my coming,
I would have added a gift in thanks for the loan.'

The Abbot did not answer.　He sat with his head cast
on his shoulder, staring at the silver rushing into hillocks
before him, as if he were a child that had never seen so
much money before.　Sir Richard, silent too now, cut
the laces of the second, third, and fourth bags, and soon
the loudest sound in the hall was that of mounting silver
coins.　The Prior had to nod to two monks, with long,
accustomed forefingers, to sort the money into piles and
count it.　When they had done their duty and pronounced the sum exact, and all the coin good, the Abbot,
rousing himself, said gobblingly to the Justice:

'Add to this the fee that I paid thee!'

But the Justice plucked at his thin beard and cackled:
'Not a penny, by Him that died on tree!　You bought my
advice as to how you should act if Sir Richard could not
pay.　But he has paid.'

'Ay,' said Sir Richard, gathering the empty leather
bags together, 'and he praises God that he has an hundred
witnesses that his lands are now his own again.'

*On to the polished oak-tree ... silver pennies began
to tinkle and tumble*

And he turned from the hall and stepped forth into a misty blue darkness, in which he found only Little John and the two horses awaiting him.   The grooms with the sumpter mules had vanished.   When he grieved that they had gone before he could thank them, and would have hastened to catch them up, Little John said, nay, 'twould be no use.   They would be too far gone already.   'Robin Hood's way,' said he.   The knight, listening to distant trotting that seemed to spell out the words 'Robin Hood! Robin Hood!' felt a whiff of magic in the air.

However, Little John, very solid and cheerful, still remained to him.   His orders, said the giant, had been to see the knight safe home to his castle in Uttersdale.

So Sir Richard at the Lee and Little John returned to the Samson Inn, where the knight had left the fine clothing given to him by Robin Hood.   Before they went to bed Sir Richard asked Little John if there was no delicacy he would fancy for supper.   Whereupon the giant squire, sitting with his hands on his knees, looking shy and childish, admitted after some pressing that if there was a taste he favoured in his mouth, last thing o' nights, it was gingerbread.   So he got that.

Sir Richard's lady met him at the gate of his castle in Uttersdale, which he reached with dusk the next day. Since his face and his new clothing were hidden from her by the darkness of the night, she cried out bravely:

'Welcome home, my lord.   Have we lost all?'

Sir Richard bent from the saddle bow and kissed her cheek, and answered: 'Be merry, dame, and pray for Robin Hood.'

Afterwards that night they were very merry, making a feast of what fare they could gather together thus

hastily.   When they had feasted in the hall of the castle,
they withdrew upstairs to my lady's solar chamber, to
sit over the fire and crack nuts and nibble sweetmeats.
The dame insisted that Little John must come up too.
She wanted him to stay with them for Christmas.   But
Little John, sitting on a carved coffer, which was the only
seat in the room large enough for him, shook his head
violently and said that he must first report to his captain.
After that, he thought of entering private service for the
dead months of winter.

'If you would enter any gentleman's service,' said Sir
Richard's dame, 'come to us.'

And all her six daughters, whose ages ranged from
fourteen to three, piped in chorus: 'Oh yes.   Come
to us, good Little John.'

But Little John, sitting with his great hands on his
knees, said very solemnly that he was not thinking of
hiring himself to any country gentleman.   He had a
mean, wealthy, town-bred employer in his mind, who
needed him sorer.   'And to him,' said he, 'I shall be
the worst servant ever he had.'

Sir Richard's six daughters were all agog to hear more,
and especially more about Robin Hood.   But when they
began to put questions their father looked stern and said
that weary men must not be plagued.   He comforted
them by promising that he would tell them the story of
his own adventure the next night.   So that night they
were simply merry and played games.   Sir Richard's
lady had got out her best dress because she was happy.
It was white velvet patterned with vines, and the
daughters' best dresses were white camlet with sky-blue
sleeves.   This gentle colouring suited them, for they had
taken after their father, and had hair light as a straw-stack

in sunshine, and innocent grey-blue eyes. The two eldest, whose names were Rosia and Aveline, were particularly happy, because now they would not have to marry two ancient merchants, who had been ready to take brides of noble birth and fair looks, even if they brought no dowries. Of the four younger sisters, two were to have been sent to a cross, sickly aunt, where they would have lived the lives of caged birds. The other two were to have entered a nunnery with their mother. Now that they were told that they might keep their animals—of which they had a great many—and stay at home, and that their dear brother would be returning, they could not stop jumping up and down for joy.

They played 'hoodman blind' with Little John, and although he was so large he was wonderfully clever at not being caught by the blind man. He leapt from table to dresser like an ape, and once, when he was almost caught, swung himself up on to the beams of the ceiling and turned somersaults. When he was made to be blind man himself, he caught three of the daughters in the first swoop of his great arms. They almost wept when he rode out of the castle gates the next morning. But he had told them that this day year their father was going again to Robin Hood's secret trysting tree to pay back the four hundred pounds. And their father was going to tell them all he knew about Robin Hood to-night. So they cheered up and began wishing it could be this day year as soon as their father had told his tale.

He told it to them up in the solar chamber and by firelight again. The six daughters of Sir Richard at the Lee looked rather like little rabbits, as they sat scattered about the floor on cushions, all pop-eyed and bursting with questions. They soon began to wish that their

mother and not their father could have been captured
by outlaws, for she could make a good story out of almost
nothing. She was quite as much interested as her
daughters, and made Sir Richard go back to the beginning
twice, and tell the tale properly, beginning with the
London-born archer in Pomfret, who had wanted to
drive a bargain for White Surrey, the steed now happily
left in Robin Hood's care for a year. Sir Richard was
willing to tell them as much as he could, now that Robin
Hood's servant, of whom it would not have been good
manners to ask questions about his master, was out
of hearing. He told them that since his first tournament
he had not felt so ill as he had done when Little John and
Much and Will Scarlet had stopped him on Barnesdale
with the greeting that he must dine with Robin Hood.
When asked to describe them, he said that Scarlet was a
Yorkshire man, he was sure, not only because the fellow
looked like one—big, square, and broad-spoken—but
because he had heard another of the band call him Scathelock, which was probably his true name and a right
Yorkshire one.

As to Much, that youth had himself told Sir Richard
during dinner that his father had been a jolly miller, own-
ing a good mill on the fringes of the forest.

'Which forest?' asked the children, thinking that they
might go on their ponies to see Much's father and hear
more about Robin Hood. But Sir Richard said that
Much had not mentioned what forest, and anyway he had
run away from home two years past. He had done this
because four of the King's officers, whose duty was to
guard the royal chases, had found Much's favourite
hound hunting, they said. They had led it away upon
a chain, and shut it up, and Much knew that the cruel

law was that any man's hound found hunting in the King's forest must lose its forepaws.   And that, he had said,

Much

was the kind of thing that made honest men turn outlaws. So he had started to run the moment they had seized his hound, and never drawn breath until he came upon Little John and Will Scarlet in the forest.   They had hurried

back with him to the forester's lodge, and knocked the
King's officers senseless, and battered down the door
of the hut in which the hound was imprisoned. After
which, said Much, he had made up his mind to be a
Robin Hood's man.

The hound, said Sir Richard, had been marvellously
ill-favoured, but Much had said that it had thought itself
in heaven now, and so did he. It was called Tomson,
and he had found it a seemly bride amongst the outlaws'
hounds, and had offered Sir Richard a puppy any time the
knight was overmuch plagued with rats.

The children lamented piteously when they heard that
their father had refused Much's offer, and their mother
said: 'Enough, enough. Dear Lord, for love of the sweet
saints, leave telling us of Much the miller's son's hound's
whelps, and get on to Robin Hood. 'Tis almost fairy-
time.'

Sir Richard, like most fathers, was ill able to describe
another man. He said that Robin Hood was of courteous
manners, well-favoured, and a goodly height.

'Of what height? As high as you, my lord, or as high
as his squire whom we had here last night?' asked his
lady.

'Well,' said Sir Richard, 'betwixt us twain.'

As to colour, he would only repeat that Robin Hood
had seemed to him to be a proper brown man in a brown
forest. In the spring, he believed, the great outlaw and
his band all wore Lincoln green to match the greenwood.
These months, they had said, were their happiest, when
the bucks were in grease, and the nights were short and
warm. They stayed in the forest some part of the winter,
he knew, for then was the best hind and doe hunting.
But Robin had told him that he had never liked slaying

these gentle creatures, and that for love of Our dear
Lady, no female creature ever suffered hurt at his
hands.

'He loves Our dear Lady best. He must be a good
man!' cried Sir Richard's pious dame. 'And has he no
good wife of his own in the greenwood, and little maids
like mine?'

'Not he,' said Sir Richard shortly.

'How do you know?' came in chorus. 'Did he say so?'

'Why nay. But I saw no sign of such.'

'Oh! I hope he has,' said the dame, and all the
daughters echoed 'I hope he has.' They thought that
they would like to play with Robin Hood's children.

'Nay,' said Sir Richard, 'I can but tell you I saw not a
kirtle in his lodge, and all the cookery for our dinner was
done by men.'

His lady asked swiftly was the cookery good. When
she heard 'Fit for King Edward,' she sighed, and said
she had feared that would be the answer. 'Still,' she
consoled herself, 'it is almost winter. Mayhap he has
a wife and children snug in some village till the green
leaves bud.'

'That the band scatters, ere Twelfth Night until the
spring tide, I can tell you,' said Sir Richard, 'for he himself mentioned that he had spent last Christmas in an
abbey by the sea. "Praying and fishing," said he with
his smile—that smile. . . . Ah! *certes*, he is a bachelor.'

'Then,' said Sir Richard's eldest daughter, clasping
her knees inside her long skirt, and staring into the rosy
caverns of the fire, 'I think that if he is yet a bachelor,
he is deeply in love with some fair maid of high degree,
and she with him, and they have plighted their troth,
but he may not claim her until he has won the King's

pardon, and got back his lands, and taken his true name again.'

'When said I ever that he was of gentle birth or had another name?' said Sir Richard.

'You spoke continually of Little John as "his squire,"' his wife reminded him. 'None but knights have squires.'

'I did. I did. Strange,' admitted Sir Richard, beating his hand on his knee.

'And you said he spoke gently, and was not mutton-fisted, like Much and Scathelock and good Little John, and that he washed and wiped ere he ate—and oh! a mort of sure signs.'

'He is a desperate captain of desperate men,' said Sir Richard, 'and the less we speak of him outside these walls, the better service we shall do him.'

'Well, for my part,' said the lady, rising, and putting away her sewing, 'I begin to think that your dear father slept in the forest and dreamed awhile. Yet hold. There is still the four hundred pounds to explain. . . . Well, mayhap Robin Hood and his merry men are not men of flesh and blood at all, but People of the Forest, like Robin Goodfellow and King Oberon. Come, children, the tale is done and your beds gape for you.'

So the children trooped off to bed, and just as she was falling asleep, the youngest daughter said out aloud: 'Little John is flesh and blood anyway.' She dreamt that night that she was in the forest, the only lady amongst many squirrels, foxes, badgers, and fallow deer. She was being wedded to Little John by the fat Friar who wore scarlet hose, and Little John said he loved ginger-bread more than knight's daughters. Suddenly a green archer, all ringed about with light, stepped from a hollow oak and cried: 'Halt there! No mortal maid can wed one of Robin Hood's men.'

But when daylight came she forgot that dream in the pleasure of seeing her only brother safe home again.

Sir Richard's heir was called Prosper, and every evening that winter, after darkness fell, he sat making arrows, beautiful arrows, winged with peacock's feathers, the best in the world to aid flight. Each was an ell long, and nocked with white silver, and he burnished their heads till they glittered in the firelight. Prosper was dark and slight, like his mother, and full of spirit, but now he spent his days riding round his father's estate, putting wrongs to right, so that they should have saved four hundred pounds by next autumn. He looked no more for angry neighbours at whom he could ride with couched lance, as of yore. His secret plan, as he confided to his fourth sister, whom he liked best, and called Pippin (for Philippa), was to have a gift of a hundred good bows and arrows ready by November to take to Robin Hood under the trysting tree. And although he was by now two-and-twenty, he was longing no less than his sisters to see Robin Hood face to face. He thought of him most of the time while he sat with his dark head bowed, chip-chipping with his dagger, or clenching his teeth while he tried bow-strings over his knee. Meanwhile his mother span, and his sisters slept, and his father held forth, like many a knight before him, how England was being brought to ruin by foreigners.

PART TWO

THE SHERIFF of NOTTINGHAM

THE Sheriff of Nottingham was a downright disagreeable
man.   People who had to have him to stay, when he rode
round the county presiding over courts of justice, which
he did every six months, said to one another, when the
date of his visit drew near, that really they didn't think
they could stand him again so soon.   But in the depths
of the country, there generally only was one house in a
neighbourhood large enough to hold him and his retinue,
and if people did not want to have him, they either had
to say that they were ill, and stay indoors and go to bed,
which was dull, or go away upon a visit themselves, which
was often inconvenient.   When his coming drew near,
country ladies would send squires galumphing on stout
nags over miles of bad roads, with letters, written for them
by the parish priest, and saying things like: 'Sweet Lady
Hawise.   God have you in his keeping.   The Sheriff
comes this day seven-night, and all my children have
fever.   Could you have him?'   Then the sweet Lady
Hawise would get into her horse-litter, or up behind a
squire on a palfrey, and come over herself to explain that
it was not possible for her to have him this year, because
her aunt was dying, or all the salt meat in her castle had
gone bad.   Sometimes, in the end, the ladies would toss
up for who should have him, and the winner would kiss
the loser at parting, and make her promise to come over
again, directly he had gone, and tell her everything that
had happened and how unpleasant he had made himself
this time.

They were seldom disappointed, for it was quite usual
for the Sheriff to greet a hostess by saying that he would
not have recognized her.   She had aged so since his last

visit. When proud parents presented their babies to
him, either they reminded him of someone else's child,
who had died young, or, if they were hopelessly perky-
looking children, he would ask them at what hour was
bedtime, and if they knew that sweets were very bad for
the teeth. When nervous pages, serving at table, said
'Malvoisie, sir?' politely offering the best wine, he would
snarl: 'Don't I look as if I were accustomed to drinking
Malvoisie?'

But it was difficult to tell when he meant to be rude,
because he always looked unpleasant, even when he was
enjoying himself. He was rather fat and pallid, and ate
enormously, and had a manor on the edge of Sherwood
Forest, and one of the finest stone houses in Nottingham
town. There he lived with his daughter, who was six-
and-twenty, and ought to have been married years agone.
But she was like her father, so no one would take her without a fat dowry. Besides, if she had married, the Sheriff
would have had to hire a housekeeper, or marry again
himself. He was the richest man in Nottingham, and
a famous pincher. Every one disliked him. However,
as folk said to one another, in these unpleasant times,
with the Scots war dragging on, and bad harvests, and a
King who was said to be weakish, and barons and clergy
who were certainly not, flying at one another like mad cats,
and outlaws in the forest, perhaps it was as well to have
an unpleasant man as the King's deputy in one's shire.

The Sheriff had, as well as presiding over courts, to
collect juries, and execute writs, and keep prisoners in
safe custody and pronounce death sentences. He was
allowed to call out the Town Guard, and as he was liable
if a prisoner escaped, it was worth his while to see that the
Guard was efficient. He was always looking out for

stout yeomen to protect him, though he liked to pretend
that he was a regular country gentleman, a great hunter,
and afraid of no man.

In the winter of the same year as Sir Richard at the Lee
paid his debt to the Abbot of St. Mary's at York, the
Sheriff of Nottingham got him a new servant, an enormous
knave, over seven feet high, and suitably broad, with soft
brown ox-eyes, and a curly black beard. The Sheriff
watched the man shooting with a party of young fellows
on a November day in the dry ditch underneath the castle.
His dull eye brightened, and he called the man up to him
and asked:

'What's your name? Where were you born, and
where do you live now?'

The man answered, bowing: 'Sir, my mother has told
me that I was born in Holderness. When I am at home,
men call me Reynold Greenleaf.' He added: 'I am
squire to a knight that will go to Palestine.'

The Sheriff growled, after looking him up and down:
'Grrmph! If you will come to me, Reynold Greenleaf,
I will give you twenty marks a year.'

Greenleaf said that he would see if his master would let
him accept this offer. Next morning he presented himself on the Sheriff's doorstep, saying that his knight had
agreed that he should enter the Sheriff of Nottingham's
service for one year. He said also, that his knight had
always provided him with a good horse, and a groom,
and the Sheriff liked the look of Greenleaf's inches and
muscles so much that he did not object. He told his
steward to take the new man up to the gallery where the
servants slept. It was empty at this hour, as they were
all about their duties, and the steward did not linger when
he had shown Greenleaf which pallet bed should be his.

Greenleaf sat down upon his pallet when the steward was gone, and set his great hands on his knees, and looked about him with a sweet smile, and said softly:

'I shall be the worst servant ever Sheriff had!'

The Sheriff's great new man was the greatest success, and soon became a familiar figure tittuping by his master's side, from court to court, all over the county. Either outlaws fled at the sight of him, or they were not what they had been, for throughout the winter the Sheriff had no trouble from them and never saw so much as the tail-feather in the cap of one. He began to say that he had ridded his district of them, and waxed bold and boastful.

Greenleaf, for his part, enjoyed all the pleasures of town life, and went with the cook at Christmas to see the mystery played in the Market Square. He laughed so loud when Noah's wife knocked down Noah, that several people turned round to see the Sheriff's great man enjoying himself. He learnt that the Sheriff's reputation for meanness was not unearned, and saw many a poor wight, kinsman of a prisoner, snivelling out of the door of the fine stone house, while his master turned back to his savoury supper. He learnt also where the Sheriff locked up the silver cups that were his pride, and how to open the secret panel in the foot of the bed where his master kept his treasure-chest.

On a fine morning in March Greenleaf woke late, and stretched himself, and remembered first that it was Wednesday and then that his master was not at home. The Sheriff had gone for a day's hunting from his manor on the edge of Sherwood. Reynold Greenleaf arose slowly, and stumbled over to a window of the gallery, and bending down—he was so tall—looked out. A maid in a blue gown was casting pails of water from an upper window of the house opposite. The street was so narrow and the top storeys of the houses in it were so close together, that he could easily have shaken hands with her. He noticed that she was a comely maid, and she winked at him for good morning, but he noticed also that the piece of sky above the roof over her head was a brighter blue than her gown, and the air smelt warm. Spring had come at last.

He put on his clothes, and went down and asked the steward politely: 'Good sir, pray give me to dine.'

Downstairs all was confusion, for the Sheriff's servants hated him well, and whenever his eye was not upon them they did as they liked, and cheated him as far as they dared. The steward, who was jealous of Greenleaf, said over his shoulder:

'You can wait for your dinner till your dear master comes home.'

Although Greenleaf was so large, the steward deemed him chicken-hearted, because he never complained of the Sheriff, like all others in this house. But to-day:

'Do you know,' said Greenleaf, fetching the steward back by an ear, 'I think I had liefer crack thy crown.'

The steward wrenched himself free and ran out of the hall. The butler, who had been standing behind him, and had sniggered when the steward had spoken so slightingly to the big man, fled for his buttery to make fast its door. But Greenleaf ran after him and gave the door a kick that brought it off its hinges. Fetching him forth by the nape of the neck, he flung him on to the stone floor of the hall, as a feaster flings a gobbet to a waiting hound. And there the butler lay, on his face, groaning, and dared not rise, while Greenleaf, seated on a cask of oysters, began to help himself to all he could lay hands upon. He washed his meal down with both ale and wine, because both were there handy.

While he was feasting, the cook appeared, with a wooden tray of open tartlets on his bare arm. When he saw Greenleaf seated on the oyster barrel, making two bites of a venison pasty, he gaped and said:

'Thou art a shrewd knave!'

He laid down the tray of tartlets on a shelf, dusted some flour off his forearms, and before Greenleaf had time to rise, dealt him three quick blows that knocked him from his seat.

Greenleaf was on his feet again in a trice, shouting: 'Those strokes like me well!' He looked at the cook, who was a square fellow, but of no great stature, and roared: 'Get thee a sword!'

The cook ran to the hall and came back with a sword, and there and then they fell to, fighting like two heroes. They fought one another out of the buttery, and up the hall, and into the courtyard behind the house. When they had fought until both were out of breath, although neither was wounded, Greenleaf shouted:

'Enough, good cook! By my faith, thou art one of the best swordsmen ever I knew. If thou couldst shoot with a long bow as well as thou canst ply thy blade, I could lead thee to a better place than this, and a better master.'

'Put up thy sword,' said the cook, and offered his hand.

After they had shaken hands and sworn eternal brotherhood, they went to the kitchen and talked, and had some more food—the Sheriff's best wine, numbles of doe, and white bread. When they had finished, Greenleaf said:

'We will be with Robin this night! But first let us get him his gift from our master here.'

THE Sheriff of Nottingham rode in the King's forest of Sherwood—the Sire-wood. Other men might not even carry bows and arrows within its glades, but he was privileged. Although the month was but March, spring had poked her head out of her bed-curtains this afternoon, and sunlight of a strength town-dwelling folk had almost forgotten, was slanting through thickets bright with pale green buds. In the distance the royal castle of Nottingham was outlined blue as a harebell against a sky full of little puffy clouds, hurrying west, and smoke of the same colour rose from many thatched roofs below it. Only the Sheriff, in his formal gown adorned with lumps of fur, looked gloomy.

He was going home after a poor day's sport, and he had lost his Fewterer, the man who looked after his greyhounds in their kennels, and both his Berners, whose duty was to keep up with his running hounds. He had taken no guests with him into Sherwood to-day, for it was too late in the season to hunt the hind and doe, and too early as yet for the hart and buck. But he liked to visit the forests out of the regular hunting seasons, because it did forest officers good to feel that the Sheriff's eye was upon them. Also he might always happen upon some poor soul unlawfully cutting the dry wood from oaks, hazels, thorns, limes, alders, and hollies. He had caught two such to-day, a ragged boy and a shaking old man, dragging after them a home-made cart on wheels. They had said that they had only picked up such branches as they had found lying, to make a fire to warm them in their hovel. He had guessed that they had meant to sell the wood in the town, and that they would never be able to pay the fine imposed for theft of the King's property. They would certainly get a whipping. All the forest officers had been cheerful, and had assured him that there had been few thieves in Sherwood all winter. There was a rumour that the band led by the man whose name the Sheriff would never mention, had moved north, into Barnesdale.

All the same, the Sheriff's heart missed a beat when he saw, coming towards him at a run, a tall man with a long bow on his back. No stranger was supposed to be in the forest at all after dark, and dusk was falling. The man came closer, and the Sheriff called out in surprise:

'Reynold Greenleaf! What dost thou here?'

The giant servant dropped on his knee and answered, pantingly: 'God save thee, dear master! I have just seen the fairest sight ever man saw in forest.'

The Sheriff was so much relieved that he forgot to press his question, and what Greenleaf told him put it out of his head entirely.

'Not half a mile away, master . . .' The man pointed wildly. 'A hart . . . leading a herd of gentle deer, to the number of seven score. There were so many of them and he had such antlers I dared not venture nearer all alone. He was no Squire, Brocket, nor Staggart, but indeed a Hart Royal.'

The Sheriff turned his horse, and Greenleaf began to run before him at a loping trot. When they had got out of sight of all landmarks that the Sheriff knew, he asked Greenleaf uneasily:

'How comest thou to know thy way so well in the King's forest?'

Greenleaf checked, laid a hand on the Sheriff's reins, and answered: 'Lo, sir! There is the Master Hart I spoke of.'

The Sheriff stood up in his stirrups, and dropped back into his saddle as if struck by a bolt. For the Hart Royal at which his servant pointed was a mortal man, dressed all in green, and leaning against an oak, so much the colour of his garments that only his bronzed face shone clearly in the rays of the setting sun. He flung up his right arm, in which was a long bow, and cried heartily:

'Welcome home, Little John! What bringest thou here?'

'The proud Sheriff of Nottingham, captain dear,' answered Greenleaf, running forwards.

The Sheriff, finding himself released, put spurs to his horse and tried to turn it in every direction. But whichever way he made to run away, a laughing man in Lincoln green stepped in his path. He called out, almost weeping with rage:

'Woe worth thee, Reynold Greenleaf! Thou hast betrayed me.'

The man whom Greenleaf addressed as captain came towards the Sheriff. He had a stately gait, and although he did not seem to hasten, he covered the ground swiftly. He said, putting back a green hood from a fox-red head:

'Good Sir Sheriff, know my face. My name is already known to you. Ay,' as the stout Sheriff shrunk back aghast, 'it is Robin Hood.'

The Sheriff of Nottingham sat under Robin Hood's trysting tree, which was thirty feet round, and was served with his dinner. When he was offered a cup of mazer wood, set in silver-gilt mounts, his eyes stood out and he started as if he had been stung by an adder. He looked up into the face of the man that offered it, and stifled an oath.

'I promised you should feast as if you were in your own home,' said Robin softly. 'All the silver cups we shall use this night are known to you. And lest you should fear lack of money so far from town, let me tell you for your comfort that we have here as well the chest from the hidel in your bed-foot, containing—how much coin was it, Friar?'

'Three hundred pounds and three, I thank God,' intoned the fat Friar, who had blessed this feast.

'Furthermore, this cook of yours has a marvellous light hand with pasties,' added Robin.

The Sheriff would not answer, or even raise his eyes again. He sat breathing hard and breaking the bread on his plate into little pieces. When Robin Hood's voice said: 'Nay now, you must make better cheer than this, sir,' he lifted a morsel to his lips, but it made him choke. He sat dumb as a fish while his host made easy gentleman's conversation. Robin Hood thought that all in Nottinghamshire should enjoy a good season this summer. Both the weather and the sport promised well. Already the deer were beginning to shed their old antlers. . . . The old stags were dropping. He spoke of spring and young men in love. This morning he had seen a gay youth clad in fine scarlet, most fantastically capering in Sherwood and hanging love-rhymes on the saplings.

The Sheriff sat with his chin sunk on his chest. When he had to answer he did no more than nod or shake his head. Presently Robin Hood asked if he would like to see a little shooting, and at that he shook his head vigorously. A devilish smile dyed Robin's lips.

'Be comfortable, dear sir,' he begged. 'I did but offer

that some of my fellows should shoot at a mark set above our heads on the tree here, while we finished our feast.'

But the Sheriff was nothing comforted by that suggestion for his entertainment.

At last Robin Hood seemed to tire of so dull a companion, and he rose to his feet. Stifling a yawn, he asked if the Sheriff was ready for bed.

'Your own man shall make you ready,' said he, and Little John stepped forward and began to unfasten the Sheriff's shoes.

The March night was chilly, and the Sheriff shook as his kneeling servant drew off his hose. When Little John raised him to his bare feet and began to help him out of his furred over-robe and unbutton his gown, the Sheriff cried out:

'But this is murder!'

'How good a master was this proud Sheriff to thee, Little John?' asked Robin thoughtfully.

The Sheriff, standing trembling in shirt and breeches, answered for Little John: 'I never did him ill!'

Little John scratched his head, and said: 'That is truth, captain. He was disagreeable, but not worse.'

'He shall lie disagreeably, but not worse, this night then,' decided Robin Hood, and ordered a fellow whom he called David of Doncaster to fetch the Sheriff a long mantle. When his men had wrapped the sorry guest in Lincoln green, fast around as the swaddling bands of an infant, leaving only the face visible, Robin Hood bade his guest good night, and trod off.

'For me, I shall sleep proudly, sir, knowing that this night the Sheriff of Nottingham wears Robin Hood's livery.'

All around the Sheriff fine young men laid their green

cloaks on the sandy soil and settled for sleep. None of them were fat, but they were evidently accustomed to sleeping on the hard ground. The Sheriff groaned and rolled from agonies upon the roots of trees to agonies upon nests of fallen acorns. He was too cold for sleep, and far too uneasy. Nor had he the faintest hopes of escape, for even if he could have moved without rousing the ring of slumbering men that encircled him, beyond them lay another ring, of fierce-looking dogs. And just behind the great trysting tree, all that night, sat men who did not attempt to sleep. The Sheriff guessed that they were sentries, and that they relieved one another at intervals, for throughout the merciless long hours he kept on hearing fresh voices. Once, when in spite of his pain and cold he was just dropping off, he heard one of them say in a low murmur:

'I favour sword and dagger at the finish.'

'But you should be able to find the heart with your arrow,' said another voice.

'They are speaking of hunting the buck,' prayed the Sheriff.

However, another voice chimed in: 'I am with Right-hitting Brand. When his head jumps at your feet, a man will not bite you again.'

Daylight began to steal into Sherwood, and slowly the scene changed from grey to green. In the budding branches overhead, birds began to twitter, and here and there a dog raised his head from between his paws, and sniffed at the fresh thin air of the new day. In Papplewick hamlet near by, in a clearing of the forest, a cock crew, and several men woke.

The Sheriff's eyes, the only part of him that moved,

shifted from figure to figure, as one by one the outlaws around him sat up, stretched themselves, and sauntered off to dip head and shoulders in a pool. They came back whistling and shrugging into their tunics, and never had the Sheriff been surrounded by so many glowing faces that he misliked. They kindled a fire and began cookery upon it. Suddenly he became aware that their captain was amongst them, bare to the waist, and trying a bow-string over his knee. The Sheriff groaned, and Robin Hood remembered him.

'Good Scarlet, pray fetch our guest his squire. He must be dight for his breakfast. Make haste, my merry men.'

Two men ran up to the Sheriff, and catching hold of a corner of the long cloak in which he lay swaddled, gave it a tug that tossed him on hands and knees into a thicket. He thought this the beginning of the end, and began to screech like a hen:

'Mercy! Mercy!'

'Peace,' cried Robin Hood, coming to stand astraddle above him, and looking down with hard chestnut eyes. 'For love of Little John thy life is granted to thee. Now get up and wash and eat.'

Little John came with a ewer and basin of ice-cold water, and laved the Sheriff's face and hands tenderly as a nurse. He went away and came back with a bundle under his arm, which proved to be the guest's hose and shoon and warm furred kirtle and over-gown. Afterwards he brought meat and ale and the Sheriff ate hungrily, and began to look more like his old self. Still he trembled when Robin Hood, tugging a belt around a tunic of Lincoln green, with long sleeves curiously tagged to resemble oak-leaves, appeared to sit beside him.

'I am glad to see that you are beginning to take to our ways, Sheriff,' said Robin pleasantly.

The Sheriff answered: 'How long will you keep me here?'

'You will scarcely learn to make a good outlaw in less than a year,' considered Robin Hood. 'In a year or two, I dare say. . . .'

The Sheriff put away his dish.

'A year or two! But one night amongst you has taken ten years off my life! I shall die of cold and hardship!'

'Summer is coming,' Robin reminded him.

'I would sooner you smote off my head this morning,' wailed the Sheriff.

'No,' explained Robin patiently, 'I have promised your life to Little John for charity.'

They ate together in silence for a little while, then the Sheriff began to plead in a hurrying, low voice:

'Let me go—for charity. And yet it need not be all charity. Think again! I could be of use to you—sitting in Nottingham town—your good friend. . . . I am Sheriff of this shire, and have powers. . . .'

Robin thought. 'You would certainly be an untoward care to me here. And I doubt if we should ever make you a bold outlaw. If I let you go, will you swear to stay my friend?'

'With all my heart,' said the Sheriff, looking up, fascinated as a cony by a snake.

'Saddle the Sheriff's horse,' commanded Robin, rising, 'and meanwhile he shall swear before us all to love us all.'

He unsheathed his sword with a whipping noise, and thrust its hilt under the Sheriff's nose.

'Lay your right hand on this, and speak after me: "By this Rood . . ."'

'By this Rood,' repeated the Sheriff, 'I swear friendship with Robin Hood, and with all his band. I will never seek to harm him by water or land. And if any of his men are brought before me, by night or by day, I will give them all the help that I may. So help me God.'

THE sound of a horse cantering away towards Nottingham town died on the air, and all the familiar noises of
a spring morning in the forest took up again.   At Papplewick the ironworker was busy with bellows and forge.

'I think my winter's work not wasted,' said Little
John.

Robin Hood did not answer, and Much glanced at his
master.   Robin was still looking in the direction whence
that rounded figure clad in black camlet and furs, and
sitting like a bundle on the back of its costly palfrey,
had grown smaller and smaller, until it had vanished
altogether.   A twig cracked, and Little John laid a
finger on the collar of Much's hound Tomson, who had
pricked his ears, and was growling softly.   Across the
glade down which the Sheriff had gone home, a man was
passing.   Robin nodded, and his two companions made
off at a run.   The stranger turned, and fitting an arrow
to his bowstring, called out:

'Stand off!' and when they halted: 'What is your will
with me?'

'Young gallant, you must come straight before our
captain under yonder tree,' said Little John, pointing.

The young gallant, who had a shock of waving dark
hair and a jutting chin, offered no more resistance, and
when he saw Robin Hood, kept his head up, and gave
him look for look.

Robin said: 'Fair young sir, did I not see thee capering
in this forest yesterday?'

'Very like,' answered the young man carelessly.
'Yesterday I may have done anything.'

Robin answered as carelessly: 'Hast thou any money about thee to spare for my merry men and me?'

'I have no money,' said the young man, 'but five shillings and a ring. You are welcome to the ring, which I have kept for seven years to use at my wedding —pah!'

'So! Yesterday you sang roundelays of love, and to-day you would fling away your bride's ring,' commented Robin.

The young man answered in bitter accents: 'Yesterday I looked to be wedded to a fair maid that I love and that loved me well. But to-day she is to be taken from me and given to be an old knight's delight. Whereby,' he added, 'my poor heart is slain.' And plucking forward a small harp which he wore slung on his back, the fantastical creature began to twang at its strings. He hopped to a fallen tree-trunk, and raising one leg upon it, set his harp on his knee, flung up his dark head, like a hound baying at the moon, and began to sing about his broken heart. He had a voice of exceeding strength and beauty, excellently trained, and his song brought creeping towards him many a green archer and the fat Friar. The Friar listened with tears streaming down his apple cheeks, and when the young man ended his song on a sudden shouting note:

'Enough, my son, enough,' said Friar Tuck. 'You remind me of many things, but particularly of a jolly hen-wife that I once knew, when I was a young clerk. She dwelt in a village called Bunny, t'other side of Nottingham on the Loughborough road, and had buried three husbands. . . .'

The young man blew his nose loudly, and looked to Robin Hood, who seemed lost in thought. All the

Friar Tuck

outlaws too looked to their captain.   At length he started, and said:

'My name is Robin Hood.'

'And mine,' said the young man coolly, 'is Alan a Dale.'

'Then, Alan a Dale,' said Robin Hood, 'what wilt thou give me if I can help thee to thy true love again?'

'I have five shillings,' said the young man.   'And if you like I will swear on a book to join your band as master of your music.'

'That will like me well,' said Robin Hood.   'Now . . . how many miles away does your true love live?'

'Only about five miles,' said Alan a Dale, 'but she is to be wedded ere noon this day.'

'This day!' exclaimed Robin Hood, and raised his horn to his lips.

The sun was high in the heavens when the marching outlaws, headed by their captain and Alan a Dale, came in sight of the village where the wedding should be.   It had rough-coated, mud-splashed cows in the water meadows around it, and gates shining silver after a spring shower, and a single street of white-and-black cottages with thatched roofs.   Its church stood outside it, on the banks of the Cocker Beck, a merry stream, bubbling full now.   The tower of the church, which rose a little apart from its new-built chancel and nave, as if it had quarrelled with them, was dove-grey against the background of budding woods.   There was a sound of lambs bleating, and in the churchyard a drift of snowdrops.

Robin Hood left his men in shelter at the edge of the forest overlooking the scene.   He said to Alan a Dale: 'Lend me thy harp,' and strode down alone towards the church.   Its porch was already filled with gaping village folk, come to see a show.   The beadle, who was armed with a whip to drive out strange dogs, told Robin that he could not enter. The church was already packed. The Bishop was here, and the bride was just coming. The Bishop himself came peering forth, and when he saw Robin, he leant on his gilded crozier, and said in querulous tones: 'What's all this? What's all this?' He was a lean, skinny Bishop, half crazy with age, with a bird's eye, and a habit of piping at you with his head aslant. His cope was sewn with saints and angels, in coloured silks and gold thread, raised as thick as your hand, and the jewels on his mitre winked at the awed country folk, who said 'Aa-ar!'

Robin Hood said, smiling his dire smile: 'My lord Bishop, I am a bold harper, the best in the North Country.'

To this the Bishop answered tremulously: 'Welcome! Welcome! I am very fond of that sort of music. Come in. Come in. You are making a draught.'

'You shall hear no music,' muttered Robin as he passed into the church, 'until I see both bride and bridegroom.'

There were no seats in the church, and the images within it were veiled for Lent. But it was light and bright, being newly built, and there was a fine painting of St. Christopher on the wall opposite the door by which Robin entered, and above that door Our Lady, lending her girdle to weigh down the good souls in the balances held by St. Michael. The foliage and moulding on the pillars were painted green and red and blue, and the floor was strewn with rushes and herbs whose odour mingled with those of wet furs and warm cloth. There had been a sharp shower just as the guests arrived.

Robin Hood made his way up to the altar steps, and

Robin Hood stepped in front . . . 'I do not like this match. April
should not wed December'

stood there looking down the aisle with narrowed eyes. He had not waited long when there was a sudden hush outside, and the sound of horses' hooves, and chariot wheels growling away. The door was flung open, letting in a fresh scurry of rain and the bride drooping on the arm of her brother, a distempered-looking youth lacking a chin. She was, as Alan a Dale had promised, a fair maid, and her long hair, sprayed on her shoulders, was glistering gold. But she was white as the snowdrops in the churchyard outside, and walked with her eyes closed as if she slept. When she reached the altar steps, where the Bishop stood waiting, an old knight with a long white beard, gnarled and crooked, but dressed out in a festival gown of black and yellow, came hobbling forwards to take his place at her side. He waved the stick on which he helped himself along, and his rheumy, red-rimmed eyes lit up at the sight of her.

Just as the Bishop was about to open his mouth, Robin Hood stepped in front of him, and after looking the bride and bridegroom up and down, said in a voice that could be heard throughout the church:

'I do not like this match. April should not wed December.'

For a moment there was silence, then a hubbub began. The Bishop tottered backwards, and the bride's brother, dropping her arm, clapped his hand to his sword. The ancient bridegroom, who was of stouter metal, drew his blade and waved it above his head, shouting in cracked accents for his men-at-arms from the churchyard outside. At that several ladies in high-collared gowns, who had been whispering to one another, burst into shrieks and made to faint into the arms of the gentlemen attending them. There was as much movement and swaying in the bright-coloured new church as in a June garden during a thunderstorm. Robin Hood put his horn to his lips and blew three blasts, even more deafening than the ladies' shrieks. Before the echoes of the third blast had died away, four-and-twenty men in green had charged downhill from the wood above, into the churchyard. They leapt its low grey stone wall and encircling stream like young deer, and all the villagers ran together for protection, calling out that the Scots had come. Some frightened horses escaped and went galloping away in the direction of the village, followed by shouting grooms. Nobody seemed eager to cross the will of an invading party, every man of which had an arrow fitted ready to his bowstring.

Half a dozen strange archers kept the church door, while into it marched a file of light-stepping men, all trim as a King's bodyguard, and alert as greyhounds. Alan a Dale, who headed them, handed Robin Hood his long bow in silence, and Robin said, looking down at the swaying congregation:

'Friends. Since we are all come to this church, we must have a wedding. But the bride shall choose her dear.'

The bride, whose eyes had never left him since he had first spoken, gave a gasp and looked past him. The first man on whom her gaze lit was Alan a Dale. She gave a single cry and would have run to hide her face in her true love's breast.

'You choose that man, damsel?' asked Robin. 'Come, Alan, you must take this maid to wife ere we leave this church.'

The Bishop came peering forwards to say: 'Here! Here! You can't do this. The law of the land is that a couple must be asked three times in church ere they are wed. That is the law.'

'Even so?' said Robin Hood. 'Then give me thy coat.'

Little John helped the flustered Bishop out of his rich vestments, and Robin Hood said to Little John: 'You put them on.' When Little John had done so, 'By the faith of my body,' said Robin Hood to his giant follower, 'these clothes make thee a man.'

At that people began to laugh. Some of the ladies present continued to shriek too, but laughter was the loudest sound as Little John strode majestically down the aisle and up again. He returned to Robin Hood, and said: 'Captain. Lest three times be not enough, I have asked these good souls seven times.' Then he said in a great voice: 'Who giveth this maid?'

'That do I,' said Robin Hood, taking her hand in his, 'and he that taketh her again from Alan a Dale shall buy her dearly.'

MAY had come, and it was warmer out of doors in the
greenwood than inside the pretty wooden house garlanded
with wild flowers that the outlaws had built for Alan a
Dale and his bride.

Alan's bride, whose name was Fair Annet, sat in the
shade of a hawthorn brake on the banks of the River
Leen. The river here formed the boundary between the
King's property and the cultivated meadows of a rich
abbey lying inside the forest. The bank on the King's
side was some three feet above the water level in summer-
time and the may-trees by which it was fringed were
loaded with spicy blossoms now, printed white as snow
against a sky of tender blue without a single cloud. Fair
Annet sat in the filtered shade of the brake, making a chain
of buttercups and daisies. She wore a gown of rosy silk,
on which the light breeze had scattered many tiny round
petals, and in the lap of her gown lay the dark head of
Alan a Dale. She asked of it:

'Husband, of what do you think so long?'

Alan a Dale, stretched at full length with closed eyes,
said dreamily: 'Of beggars, my pearl.'

'How ugsome a thing to ponder so long on such a fine
morning,' said Fair Annet. She asked with equal calm:
'Shall we be beggars when the summer is gone, Alan a
Dale?'

'Not we,' said Alan, opening his eyes, and winking at
the bright heavens above him. 'Robin Hood pays his
men forty marks a year, in season and out. When winter
comes, you and I shall wander south and dwell softly in

fair cities. There I shall learn all the latest ballads and
you shall mark the fashions until the woodweele sings
again on the spray.'

'How many seasons has Robin Hood led this life?'
asked Annet.

'I met him first on the same day that you did, only
three hours earlier, my dappled fawn,' answered Alan a
Dale, closing his eyes again.

'Ay, but you are a man, and hear men's talk,' said
Annet. 'Of what do you speak when you take your turn
as a sentry over his camp-fires in the midnight?'

'Of ban-dogs and bowstrings and beeves and beggars,
my beauty,' answered the poet.

'Tell me of your beggars then,' said Annet.

'There were three of them, attending a single mule,'
said Alan, 'and Scathelock and Brand and I met them
while you were sleeping the sleep of innocence this dawn.
We stopped them and bade them unload their wares and
hand over all silver. One of them—a very poltroon—
ran away shrieking "Murder!" The second pulled out
his dagger, but was disarmed by Scathelock and fled
silently. The third of them, left alone, hastened to spread
his cloak on the turf and unload the mule. The cloak
had many a patch of red and blue and black in it, and he
asked us to fasten down its corners while he fetched the
money bags. The sack he brought from his beast was
heavy. It was in truth filled with meal, which he,
standing between us and the breeze, emptied straightly
into our eyes. Having thus blinded us, he seized his
staff, which he had planted in the ground, gave us each
a sore blow on the head, and then made away at the gallop
after his companions.'

'Sweetheart!' cried Annet, jumping so that Alan's

head rolled on to the sward. 'You might have been slain while I slept! Where did the beast bruise you?'

'He was no beast, but a stout and jolly companion, and I would we had him in our band,' said Alan.

'Would you take for companion one that has sought to murder you?' asked Annet.

'*Certes*,' said Alan, sitting up and feeling his brow. 'It is Robin Hood's way. Is it not, Friar?'

The fat Friar, who would have passed by noiselessly after giving them a smiling blessing, seated himself gladly beside them in the lush grass, and answered cheerfully: 'Even so. I sought to slay Robin Hood at our first encounter.'

'That must have been many years ago,' said Annet, looking at his shape.

The Friar's jollity faded, and he said: 'It was more seasons past than I care to remember.'

Annet gave her husband a dig, but he said, without taking any notice of her: 'Will you tell my wife of your first encounter with your captain, Friar?'

'Oh that,' answered Friar Tuck readily, 'is a merry tale.' He unhitched his gown from its belt, and smoothing it primly to cover his scarlet legs, began. 'My poor mother (whose soul God pardon) vowed me to the church at my birth. I was a bird ill-suited to life in a cage, and I suffered many things ere I met Robin Hood. But of these we need not talk. Know only that for seven years, after I came into Yorkshire, I was guardian of the ford below the Abbey in Fountains Dale, and lived in a hermit's cell, a most solitary life. Wherefore I was glad, one May morning, as I watched by the ford, to see coming towards it a proper young gallant with a bow on his back, and at his belt a sheaf of arrows. When he came close enough for speech, he called out to me: "Good morning, good fellow. Can you tell me where I shall find the Friar of Fountains Dale that is so strong i' the arm?" I was wearing my frock tucked up, and a cap of steel over my tonsure, and a broadsword and buckler by my side (which became me well), so he might not have guessed that I was the man he sought. I said simply: "Do you desire to cross the river to find him, young sir?" "I do," said he, "and when I have found him, to match my strength against his." He said to me, like a lord: "Are you ferryman here? Where is your boat?"

'I answered, bowing low: "We keep no boat here, young sir, but if you truly desire to meet the strong Friar of Fountains, I will carry you across this ford to the Abbey."

'He hesitated but a moment, then leapt on my back, crying: "Carry me over this water, or thy life's forlorn!"

'As I felt him light as a leaf on my back, I chuckled to myself at the thought that such a one would match his strength against mine. However, much liking his spirit, I bore him safely across the river, and set him on his legs on the further side, amongst the noble yew-trees there. Now, thought I, as he slid from my back, will the sport begin. I straightened myself, and although I was no taller than he, I was twice as broad, besides bearing heavy arms. I said to him pleasantly: "Now, my fine stripling, if you would match your strength against that of the stout Friar of Fountains Dale, begin by carrying him back across this river."

'He measured me with his bold brown eye, then bending low, cried: "Mount then, stout Friar!"

'I straddled towards him, thinking, mark you, to send him sprawling the moment I lowered myself on

'*As I felt him light as a leaf on my back, I chuckled to myself . . .*'

to his back. But to my surprise, although he was so light, he was taut as a bowstring. He gritted his teeth as he hitched my legs under his arms, then crying out "Sit tight!" plunged towards the waters of Skell. Halfway across he staggered, and I prepared to catch him a buffet. He hitched me higher on his back and made on. When we got to the further side I scrambled down and waited to have the pleasure of listening to his breath coming short. But he had enough left to call out: "Carry me again over these waters, thou stout Friar, or it shall breed thee pain."

'This time I kept not to the ford, but turned directly into deep water, and Skell was full after the spring rains. When I was up to my armpits, I shook him off, saying: "Choose now whether you sink or swim." He could swim like a fish, indeed better than I, in my tucked-up frock and heavy arms. Nevertheless, he had but the use of one arm, since he must hold his bow on high, out of the water.

'When I came to rest, with my fingers round the branch of a tree overhanging the banks of Skell, I saw him just landing, a little further downstream, by a bush of brier. He fitted an arrow to his bowstring, and let fly at me as I struggled ashore. I put his arrow by, with my buckler, and went for him with my broadsword. He danced away behind a bush, and a second arrow glanced off my steel cap. So we played, like children, while the day advanced, he continually evading me and shooting at me, and I rushing at him to cut him down. He was fleet of foot and twice led me over hillocks whereupon I tripped, although I should have known that bankside better than he. Presently I knew that the day was mine, for I saw that he had used the last of his arrows and was getting out his sword. He wielded it well, but in the end, as must be, I brought him to his knees. Then he called out: "A boon, a boon, stout curtal Friar. I beg it on my knee. Grant me leave to set my horn to my mouth and blow three blasts."

'"Blow till your eyes fall out," answered I comfortably. For the fields around were empty as a beggar's larder, the hour being four of the afternoon, and all souls at their meat.

'He set his horn to his lips, and blew three blasts, with more strength than I had dreamt still dwelt in him after our battle. Neither had I dreamt that in answer to them should come, raking over the lea, half a hundred yeomen clad in Lincoln green and with bows bent. I forgot all about our feud, and cried out in simple amazement: "Whose men are these that come so hastily?" "Robin Hood's men, Friar," said he, smiling. "What wilt thou do now?" I thought swiftly, and said: "Grant me a boon now, Robin Hood. Give me leave to set my fist to my mouth and whistle thrice."

'He answered: "I should be to blame to refuse. Besides, I should like to see a fat Friar whistle."

'I stretched my mouth by putting both my littlest fingers in its corners—thus,' the Friar showed his audience, 'and I blew thrice—thus. And even as now,' said the Friar, affectionately patting the head of a hound that had come flying towards the party seated in the hawthorn shade, 'my loving troupe of ban-dogs came in answer. Only on that occasion fifty came, whereas now I have but a poor dozen.'

'Mercy, Friar!' shouted Alan a Dale, leaping to his feet and flinging an arm round his bride, as dogs came pouring towards them from all directions out of the forest. 'Call off your men!'

'You are fainter-hearted than was Robin Hood,' smiled the Friar, 'although now I give my men the order to sit. Sit! Sit!' he cried, and all the dogs flopped around him in a circle.

'Robin Hood's men,' he continued, 'when they saw my band, fitted arrows to their bowstrings, for the grandsire of Hodge here had torn Robin's mantle of Lincoln green clean off his shoulders, and Blanche, his mate—God rest her soul—nigh had his sleeve out.'

'And what was the end of it?' asked Fair Annet, cautiously reseating herself.

'Marry,' said Friar Tuck, 'the end of it was that I became Robin Hood's man, from that hour forward. For Little John called out to me to take up my dogs or he would take me up. In earnest he loosed off an arrow at Hodge, which the skilful beast, as I had taught him, caught sideways in his jaws. Then I called out: "I will hold up my men if you will hold up yours, sir squire. Your master and I, I see, must be friends, for he is the best and boldest man ever I have met. Seven long years have I kept the ford at Fountains, and never knight, lord, nor earl has ever heard me cry "Enough."'

'So we settled it, there and then, on the banks of Skell that spring afternoon, and Robin showed me how he needed a chaplain for his host, and offered me ten shillings as my fee for every Sunday throughout the year, and new apparel every holy day. I did not think that he could keep his word, for it was a prince's offer. But I liked the look of him. Nevertheless, I was wrong in my doubts. And I never,' said Friar Tuck, shaking his head as he felt the muscles of his rounded forearm, 'have

regretted my choice, although look you, I have become
just what I swore I never should, which is a fat fellow
better to sing a psalm than fell an enemy.'

Out of the forest depths came a sound of mournful
singing. The fat Friar laid a finger on his lips, and
Alan a Dale's arm stole round his wife's waist.

'Shall we go see, or go back?' he asked the Friar
softly.

The Friar advised: 'On—to see—but softly. Your
dame is safe enough thus nigh our camp.'

In a clearing close to the river's bank, two sleek black
horses were tied by their bridles to a tree. They grazed
incuriously, whilst, in front of them, kneeling in a circle,
three figures in long gowns chanted as if they were in
church. Their words, which they sang over and over
again, were: 'Money! Money! Send us, oh send us,
some money to serve our needs!'

Two of them were black monks. Their faces were
heavy and pale from cloister life and large feeding, and
they glanced at one another out of the corners of their
eyes as they kept up their strange prayer. The third
amongst them wore the gown of a mendicant Friar.
Its hue had once been brown, like the robe of Robin
Hood's fat chaplain, but it was tattered and faded until
it was scarcely to be called of any colour. His hood,
which this Friar wore pulled well forward, shaded a
bronzed throat. Although they were two to one, the
black monks were evidently in awe of the brown Friar,
and looked to him as their leader, for whenever he
turned his hood towards them they sang louder. When
he ceased to chant, and rose to his feet, they hastened
to follow his example. Fair Annet and her husband,

at a sign from Friar Tuck, halted, well hidden by the lower branches of a great oak, and waited to see what should happen. They were close enough to hear quite clearly the unctuous accents of the lean mendicant who, standing with his back to them, addressed the fat, black-frocked pair.

'And now, O my brothers, who have no money, let us search again and see what Heaven has sent us in answer to our prayers.'

The monks searched their pockets, and both replied: 'Alas! Friar, we still have nothing.' 'As we told you before,' said one, 'ere you stopped us we were robbed this morning.' 'By outlaws,' explained the other.

'But, brothers,' said the Friar earnestly, 'since then you have helped me to pray for a miracle. Let us search one another. That may be more fruitful.'

At that they groaned anew, as well they might, for in this new search, though neither of them found anything in the Friar's pockets, when he got to work on them, silver pennies began to rain from his lean fingers. Each of the black monks was wearing on a belt inside his cloak a dozen leathern bags bursting full of treasure.

'Heaven has answered our prayers bravely,' commented the Friar, coolly relieving them of their belts and flinging them on the ground at their feet. 'Since we promised one another before we prayed to share what should be sent, here is one bag of coin for each of you. Now,' he raised his voice, 'take your steeds. Like yourselves, they lack spirit.'

They made no attempt to recover their property, though as they untied their horses their sighs were deep. Just as they were about to move, the Friar stalked towards them.

'Stay! I have one more thing to say to you. You shall be sworn,' and he looked down at the sward of the clearing, littered with silver pennies, 'sworn by this holy sward, never to tell lies again. Also that when ye meet a poor man ye shall show him charity.'

The anxious pair swore gobblingly, eager to be gone.

'Farewell,' cried the Friar as they mounted, 'and when you meet your Abbot don't forget to tell him that you met a holy man who could work miracles.'

He cast back his hood with a sudden gesture as they trotted away, and the head he uncovered was no shaven crown, and glinted fox-red in the rays of the setting sun. When he had done waving to the departing figures he called over his shoulder into the dimness behind him:

'Dame! Tuck! Alan! Lend me your wits here. I reckon that between coin and jewels these friends have left us nigh on four hundred pounds.'

HE was a master of disguises, said Much (who, despite his wooden appearance, could sometimes be persuaded to talk), and he kept, hanging up in his secret forest lodge, on a rail, a dozen costumes in which he had deceived the world.   Most of them, Much believed, he had bought from their owners in the forest or on the open roads, at hours when he had needed them.

Fair Annet, who had a woman's curiosity, longed to see the market-wife's gown of striped blue-and-white stuff in which Robin Hood had ridden into Nottingham town and sold poultry for good prices at Hen Cross. (Next day, said Much, three sons of a widow who had been condemned to death by hanging, for stealing the King's deer, had escaped from the dungeons under the castle, no man knew how.)

There was a butcher's outfit in the lodge, said Much, and a palmer's (with a big flopping hat and a long staff), and a tinker's, and a tanner's.   This last smelt outrageously.   There was also, complete with horn, belt, and surcoat, all adorned with crowned E's, the full feast-day uniform of a ranger of His Grace's royal forests, a thing that could scarcely have been bought.   There was a potter's habit, much stained with clay, lying rolled up in a basket containing a potter's wheel and two grievously misshapen beakers.   As for the Friar's frock, with hood, beads, and sandals, Annet herself had seen him wearing it.   Much believed this to be one of Robin's favourite disguises, simple to don and easy to work in.   But he had only once met his master at work—attired as a shepherd, piping musically to a flock which bore every mark of belonging to a garth of the Priory of Beauvale. How he had come by the sheep, for what purpose, and how he had got rid of them again, Much had no idea.

He would not tell Annet much about the Scotsman's dress, which, he said awfully, was bloodstained and much rent by daggers, nor about the sailor's, which had attached to it a fishing line, and all the tackle that a hungry fugitive might need for a meal on the deep seas. It was quite impossible for him to take Annet in to see them—all hanging up in dimness, looking like ghosts of their past owners, with dusty hats aslant and broken toes pointing. He tried to put her off by telling her that they were indeed a poor show for a lady, and to tell truth, Robin himself took no great account of them. The marvel was that when he put one on, he put on, too, the very voice, face, and gait of its old master. Without him inside them they were just a few dirty rags. He said, too, that Robin disliked disguising himself, and only did so when he must.

This seemed true, for the very next morning Annet heard Little John and Will Scarlet grumbling about their master's project of going into Nottingham, quite openly, to attend Whit-Sunday morning service—Matins and Mass—in St. Mary's Church. He was being, said Will, as obstinate as my Lord Abbot's mule. Much had asked to go with him, taking twelve armed men. He had refused any escort, and said that he meant to go unarmed himself.

'But that,' said Little John, 'he shall not do, for I have cunningly challenged him to a shooting match, at dawn, on the edge of the forest. Thus, when he steps on to Nottingham, he shall at least bear with him his good yew bow.'

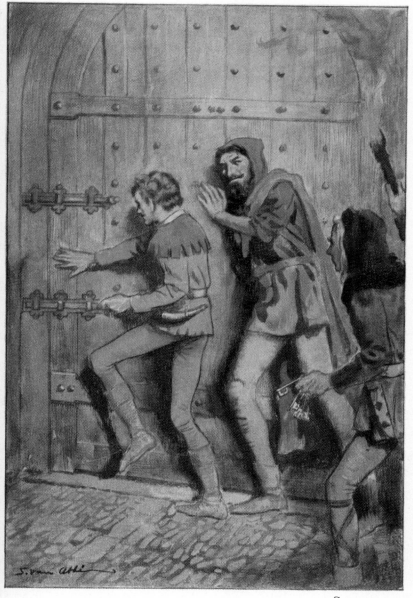

See page 100

'Lock up fast!' commanded Robin, and Little John put his shoulder
to the door again

'I wish he would take broadsword and dagger too,' said Will Scarlet.

'Well,' said Little John, 'I will carry with me to our trysting place two broadswords. And whichever of us is victor at the shooting, I mean to challenge my master immediately after to a bout of sword play. Thus I may even hold him in the forest until Matins are over.'

But at noon the next day Little John alone returned to the lodge in a very ill humour. He had won five shillings from Robin, shooting for pennies, but Robin had refused his challenge to a further trial of skill with the broadsword. He had said 'Nay,' very shortly, and set out at a brisk pace towards the town, from which church bells could be heard calling. When Little John had gone after him, importuning him, he had caught his trusty follower a buffet, and finally taken him in his arms and flung him full length on the sward. Although Little John had advantage in weight and height, no man of his band could wrestle as skilfully as Robin Hood.

'So,' said Little John, 'he has gone. And were he not my captain, I would have pommelled him sore for that buffet. Now, if he is recognized and taken in Nottingham town, he has but himself to blame. I have done all a man could do to stay him.'

Will Scarlet was hopeful that even if the worst came to the worst and Robin was captured by the Town Guard, the Sheriff, when he was brought before him, would remember his oath and let him go free. He pointed out too, that the church of St. Mary lay in the English borough of the town, where all inhabitants wished Robin Hood well. Further west, around the castle, which had been built by the first Norman King, most of the people were 'foreigners,' descendants of the

Conqueror's followers, established by him to wax rich trading in English malt and wool.

Dusk of Whit-Sunday came, without bringing home the captain to Sherwood. Still, few of his band were uneasy, for it was often his custom to disappear for days together. Next morning, however, Much came to Little John, and said that he was thinking of paying a visit to his uncle that dwelt at Sneinton, a village just outside the walls of Nottingham, on the south-east. He knew that before now, when he had put the town in an uproar, Robin had lain safely in Sneinton until the trouble had blown over. There were in this village many curious caves, hollowed out of the sand-stone, as good hiding-places as those in the castle rock. Wise mothers would not let their children play near them, for strange tales were told of them, the last of which were that they were full of bones and ghosts of Danes.

Little John, who could settle to neither sport nor work, offered to accompany Much, and they set out, telling no one of their purpose. They took food with them, gave the town a wide berth, and dined on some common land outside the walls where the causeways were built high against Trent floods. Between two bites at a doe-pasty, Little John said, staring mournfully at the distant outline of the high castle on its rock: 'For all that passed yesterday, I would I knew whether Robin lies in there thinking to himself: "Now lack I Little John!"'

They came into Sneinton after dark, and found Much's uncle taking his ease, unbuttoned in front of his fireside, alone, for he was a single man. When he saw two figures in Lincoln green on his doorstep, he made haste to draw them in and bolt the doors after them. He was by trade a carpenter, and in appearance not unlike Much, being short, broad, and platter-faced. Like his nephew, too, he was by no means as simple as he looked. He gaped at his guests as he said: 'Mild Mary! What brings you two merry men here at such an hour? Your master is ta'en,' said he, blinking at them in the firelight.

Much laid a hand on the arm of Little John who, on hearing this news, had given a roar and was for dashing out into the darkness with drawn sword.

'Softly, good giant. Fifty of your stature could not fetch Robin Hood forth from where he lies now,' said the carpenter.

'Tell us swiftly how he came to be taken,' said Much.

'I heard it first from my neighbour, the cooper's widow, a clattering woman to whose talk I pay no great heed,' said the carpenter. 'She comes too often to waste my time, with a joint stool that hath broken a leg, or a burst taper-box wrapped inside her cloak. But yesterday she brought nothing to be mended for charity, and was only agog to tell me that as she had gone into the town by the Goosegate she had met the handsomest gallant on middle earth. He was, she said, dressed in a fine suit of Lincoln green, with a broadsword by his side, a long bow on his back, and on his brave breast a silver medal of St. Christopher.'

'She spoke truth,' groaned Little John. 'He did wear his silver Christopher yesterday. Praise God he took also his broadsword.'

'He was coming as though from the Market Place,' said the carpenter, 'and stepped past her down Bridle-smithgate.'

'And I begged him,' lamented Little John, 'if he must go to St. Mary's Church, to approach like the hind going to feed her calf, softly and deviously.'

'Well, I took small account of her tale,' said the carpenter, 'for she is ever talking of handsome men. "'Tis a pity," said I to her, "that you went not up to the church to pray beside so fine a fellow." "I could not, because I had business with a dame in Houndsgate, and had to get back here for my dinner," said she. "But I can promise you I was fain." She went off, smiling foolishly, and an hour later, to my wrath, I saw her coming again to deafen me. But this time I did listen, for before I could make indoors she had cried out: "Good neighbour! Good neighbour! I was right. That was Robin Hood bowed to me in the town to-day, and now the poor young fellow is taken prisoner, and lies in irons in the nethermost castle dungeon."

'Presently a crowd gathered round us, to hear how she had met Robin Hood, for it was true enough that he had ventured himself into the town, and been taken prisoner, after a great affray in which, they say, he slew twelve men.'

'He would! He would!' groaned Little John.

'He fought like a madman, they tell,' said the carpenter. 'And mad he must have been to go into Mary's Church on a feast day, seeing how our Sheriff loathes his name.'

'He had the Sheriff's oath—given on the Cross—that he should be safe,' said Little John. 'And he trusted it. Let me meet that false man!'

'But,' said the carpenter, 'from what I hear, it was not the Sheriff raised the alarm and brought out the Town Guard. It was a black monk. Your master, after my neighbour saw him, went, it seems, up to Mary's Church, where he attended both Matins and Mass. Beside him in God's house knelt a great hooded monk. A black heart as well as a black frock must he have had, for when he had peered in Robin Hood's face and satisfied himself, he gathered up his skirts and slipped from the place. He ran fast as he might to every gate of the town, crying that the King's felon was in the church of St. Mary. Not until the warders had made fast every bar did he hie him to the Sheriff, with the tale that the worst outlaw of the North Country was within his grasp. "I have spied the foul fellow as he stood at the Mass," said the monk. "The service will be long, and he suspects nothing. His traitor name is Robin Hood, and he once robbed me of a hundred pounds. I have never," said he, "put his face out of my mind."

'The Sheriff arose and armed him, as he must, and many a mother's son ran with him up to the church. His Guard knocked with their staves on the doors, crying: "In the King's name!" But they had no great task to find Robin Hood, for he ran out amongst them, waving his broadsword, and with it he slew twelve men and wounded many more. At last he broke his blade — as Fate would have it — on the Sheriff's steel cap.

'"God work woe to the smith that made thee!" cried he, flinging away its hilt. He plunged back into the church, and there was taken, weaponless.

'Now the monk who spied him has claimed the honour of carrying to the King at Westminster, the Sheriff's letter, telling His Grace that Robin Hood, the worst outlaw in England, lies in irons in Nottingham town, awaiting His Grace's pleasure.'

'Did the monk even so?' asked Much. 'And when did he set out?'

'They tell in the town that he is not yet gone,' said the carpenter, 'and that the Sheriff, greatly fearing an attack by Robin Hood's men on the walls, has sent to

Tickhill for more soldiers. Wherefore you twain will do well to lie low awhile.'

'We shall put you to small pains for a lodging while this monk is about his work,' said Much. 'Tell me, do not the windows of the upper chamber of this house look out behind upon the high road to Bridgford, to Ruddington and the south?'

'You know they do,' said the carpenter.

'Then, good uncle, grant my fellow and me leave to repose ourselves in your upper chamber a few hours,' said Much. 'And since we shall be stirring early, give me your blessing now.'

The skies were growing light for dawn above the village of Sneinton, and still two hard-eyed men watched in vain from an upper window of the carpenter's house that overlooked the road to the south. Downstairs, in front of a dying fire, Much's uncle slept soundly.

'I vex me,' muttered Little John, 'with the thought that our bird may have flown past while your uncle told his tale. I know I was roaring like a bull most of the time. He may easily have flitted past without our knowledge, or taken another way.'

'Have patience a little longer,' urged Much, 'and I promise you that you shall have him for your part while I deal with his guards.'

'You can leave all such business to me,' said Little John. 'Blanch as he may, this stag shall not escape me.' He rose from his knees to stretch his great arms rafter-high.

When he did this he rose out of sight of the road, and it was in that moment that Much stiffened. Out in the grey world there was a sound of trotting hooves.

'Good tidings!' whispered Much, rising too. 'I can see his wide hood, and he rides alone, save for a little page. Downstairs softly, and greet him fair. He is a large man and well mounted.'

'Praise God for that,' said Little John.

An outside staircase gave access to this upper chamber, and the two watchers got down it quickly. When the black monk drew near they waved to him in friendly manner, and cried out to ask whence he came, and if he could give them any tidings of a false outlaw, Robin Hood, taken prisoner yesterday.

'We twain know him well, for he once robbed our master of twenty marks,' explained Little John, standing up straight in the dawning light, the very picture of a bold knight's squire.

The monk, who had eyes like hot coals in a cavernous face, drew rein and answered them, saying: 'It is true, praised be God, that Robin Hood is taken. And you may thank me,' said he, with his breath hanging like smoke on the cold morning air, 'that this is so, for I was the first to lay hands on him. I also have suffered wrong from him. But the sum of which he robbed me was far greater than your master's loss, good fellows.'

'I pray God to reward you, brave holy man,' said Little John. 'May we run beside you as your guardians until you come to Ruddington? The Sheriff should have given you a guard thus far, for the outlaws will be rising when they hear that their master is taken.'

'The Sheriff of Nottingham is too much feared for his own skin to spare a man from his town,' said the monk. 'I shall be glad of your company.'

About a mile further on, where the road ran between mosses and boulders covered by ling, and was very lonely, Much muttered to Little John: 'Now!' Little John pulled the monk's hood down over his face, and sprang at the head of his horse, and pulled the monk out of his saddle.   A dagger glinted in the rays of the rising sun, and the little page ran away bleating when he saw what was toward.

At nine o'clock, on an evening more than a week after Robin Hood had been taken prisoner, two late-faring travellers knocked up the warder at the Houndsgate of Nottingham town.

When the warder challenged them, they said that they rode on the King's business to the Sheriff, and they showed him a letter bearing the royal seal. The warder made haste to unbar his gate, and as they passed in, the travellers asked him: 'What is the cause that all ways into your town are barred?'

'Marry,' said the warder, 'because in a dungeon of our castle lies Robin Hood, the great outlaw. And every day of this week our walls have been assaulted.'

'By whom?' asked the travellers.

'Marry,' said the warder, 'by some great knaves of Robin Hood's band. They are all of more than mortal size, and the worst of them is called Little John, and others are named Much and Will Scarlet.'

'Even so?' said the travellers in tones of amazement, and after inquiring the way to the Sheriff's house, pressed their tired beasts on.

The Sheriff was still up, for he was an uneasy man these days, and he had been seeking to drown his anxieties in wine. When he heard that messengers from Westminster were come, he was so glad that he leapt to his feet to greet them. Since he had already drunk too much, he stumbled and fell back into his seat again. This suited his guests very well, for one of them did not desire that the Sheriff should stare into his face. Little John stayed in the shadows by the door, and left the talking to Much. 'We are lucky,' he whispered to Much, when he saw the Sheriff stumble. 'Maybe,' answered Much, 'but I have known men full of wine increased in obstinacy.'

He stepped forwards, bowing featly, and handed to the Sheriff the letter with the great seal on it, saying: 'From His Grace the King at Westminster, to the Sheriff of Nottingham.'

The Sheriff put off his hood in reverence of the King's hand and seal, and as he cut the silks which fastened the parchment, he asked: 'Where is the monk that took my letter to the King?'

'His Grace has taken such a fancy to him,' said Much, 'that he has kept him in London at his side. He is to be Abbot of Westminster.'

'Is that so?' said the Sheriff. 'Then will he be a great lord.'

'The King was so pleased,' said Much, 'to hear of Robin Hood's capture that he could not honour too much the man that was the sole cause of it.'

The Sheriff snorted. 'Did the monk boast so largely? My men took Robin Hood.'

He opened the letter, and as he read it Much said aside to Little John: 'We shall do no good here.'

He was right, for when the Sheriff had read, he announced: 'Yeoman of the Crown, for so I read in this letter that you are, His Grace writes that never was there man in Merry England he was so fain to see as Robin Hood. Wherefore I am to dispatch him to London under guard. For which God be thanked.'

'So we wotted well,' said Much. 'For His Grace said the same things to us. We will set out this night with the prisoner.'

Little John

'Nay, forsooth,' said the Sheriff. 'Ye shall do no such thing. For I am responsible for this outlaw, and all the roads around this town are beset by his felon followers. They would certainly fall upon you in an effort to bring him off. Go seek your beds. It may be a week before I have gathered sufficient force to carry Robin Hood south.'

And since he deemed his troubles not yet over, the Sheriff helped himself to another cup of wine. He had the grace to offer his guests the same, and for the space of half an hour they sat drinking with him, Little John keeping his hood well pulled down over his brows. In vain Much declared that the King was so eager to see Robin Hood that he would be wrath if they waited another week before setting forth. 'I know,' said the Sheriff, 'that he would be far more wrath if by any neglect his great enemy escaped on the road to him.' At length he fell asleep in his chair, and Much and Little John arose very softly and stole out of his house.

'Now,' said Much, when they were without, in the clear light of a full moon, 'we are little better off than we were before we went to that weary London. For this false Sheriff means to break his word to our dear master. There will be nothing for it but for us to raise all Sherwood and surprise the party that takes him south. By the grace of God we shall have some days for preparation.'

'I don't agree with you,' said Little John, 'for the King's seal has got us into this town, which all our fellows have been seeking by force to enter for a week. I wish you could have got that seal again from the Sheriff. It would have been of use to us this night.'

'He fell asleep with it in his paw,' complained Much. 'Where are you hastening?'

'Up to the castle to see our dear captain,' said Little John, quickening his pace, so that Much had to run alongside, and had no more breath for further questions.

Little John led the way through many narrow alleys and up and down stone stairs, light-footed as a cat. They met several cats on their silent passage, but never a human soul, though they often heard snores arising from the windows under which they flitted like shadows. Presently they came out into an open space, where there was a ditch covered with long grass and brambles, and Little John fell on hands and knees and began to search up and down it like a hound snuffing to find a cony's burrow. There was a dark mass of masonry behind him, and Much guessed that they were between the town wall and the castle rock. He opened his mouth to question Little John, but the giant, turning swiftly, clapped a hand over Much's mouth, and with his free arm pointed at the heavens above them. Much looked up, and saw, outlined against a sky full of stars, the figure of a man with a bow in his hand. They were indeed at the foot of the castle rock, and the man on the height behind them was a watchman of the town walls. After that, Much did no more than follow Little John like an obedient child, told to keep close to its mother's skirts in a crowd. It was lucky for him that he kept so close, for suddenly he fell sideways into space and darkness. He had found the mouth of the cave in the castle rock for which Little John had been searching. It had been overgrown by leafy bushes, for the month was May.

A moment later Little John was beside him, pulling him on to his legs and shaking him into silence. Much had uttered as he fell, and had sent some stones scattering down against the foot of the wall. A voice called out

They were . . . at the foot of the castle rock

sharply: 'Halt! Who goes there?' and the two outlaws crouched together in utter darkness while a man could have counted a score. But the watchman did not cry again, and at length Little John stirred, and felt his way past Much, and began to climb on hands and knees into close-smelling blackness. Much felt sandy soil beneath his feet, and putting up a hand, met the chill and roughness of wet stone. He knew that the castle rock was a rabbit warren of secret passages, and he guessed that Little John was leading him towards the dungeons under the keep. When he was beginning to feel that they must have travelled a mile, turning this way and that, bumping into corners, and more than once stepping into puddles, suddenly they halted, and he heard Little John fumbling as if with the handle of a door.

Little John stepped back—on to one of Much's feet —and said in a low grumbling voice: 'Bolted on the inside. But the wood is crazy. Stand away, and let me run at it.'

So Much flattened himself against the walls of the passage, and the giant outlaw came past him at a run, crouched together, and flung himself at the nail-studded door. There was a noise of splintering and the door rocked inwards, its bolt having parted company with much rotten timber. They scrambled through, and saw above them a long flight of stone steps, at the head of which arose an archway lit by unseen torches. Outlined against the tawny glare stood a peering man with a bunch of keys at his belt.

'Stay where you are and hail him!' commanded Little John, so Much stayed where he was and called out gently, raising strange echoes: 'Master Warder!' The man came two steps down towards them into gloom.

In the same moment Little John, who had crept on silently, caught him round the legs and flung him down the stairs, nearly oversetting Much. The man gave one groan and then lay still.

'Hit his head and will keep silence awhile,' announced Much. 'I have his keys.'

'Come on then,' urged Little John from on high.

'Fair enough, but which way?' panted Much, for the archway above them gave access to passages leading right and left, lit by bunches of torches stuck into brackets nailed to the walls.

'How should I know?' replied Little John crossly.

They had raised noise, bursting the door and felling the jailer, and overhead now they heard heavy footsteps. Suddenly Little John lifted up his voice and hallooed: 'Help here! Robin Hood has escaped!'

A man buckling on his sword, closely followed by another donning his steel cap, came running round the circular staircase from the Guard Room above. The first soldier called to Little John: 'Which way has he fled?' 'Down yonder into blackness,' answered Little John, drawing back to let the man charge past him. The second soldier followed his leader, but a third, who had either more wit or less courage, turned down the passage in which the outlaws were waiting. He was going to see if it were true that their bird had flown. He reached at length a certain door on which he thundered, but being but an archer he had no keys to open it. Much's heart leapt as a sleepy voice called out from within:

'Sweet St. Christopher! What's ado now?'

'Whoever's escaped, 'tis not Robin Hood,' said the archer.

'Best make certain. He is a prince of feigners,'

grunted Little John, busy with the keys Much had stolen from the fallen warder's belt.

The door creaked wide, aided by Little John's foot, and the archer stepped down two steps into Robin Hood's prison, taking to light him a torch from the bracket on the wall outside. For a second they all had a vision of a tawny-headed man, with fetters on wrists and ankles, raising himself on an elbow and yawning at them. Then Little John caught up the archer as if he were a toddling child, and cracked his skull against the stone wall of the dungeon. With the archer fell his torch, and they had no light left but that which haloed the half-closed door, guarded by Much against new-comers.

'Bravely done,' commented a calm voice from the pallet in the corner of the cell. 'Now loose me to do my part.'

Little John relieved Much at the door, and Much, dropping on his knees, used the keys he had stolen on the padlocks at Robin Hood's wrists and ankles. When he felt himself free, Robin bounded from his pallet, and stretched his cramped arms to the roof, crying: 'Hola!'

Mailed men were hurrying down the passage towards them. Little John dropped from behind the door on to the neck of the first man that entered, and Robin Hood caught the second round the waist and flung him on to the pallet bed, careless as a man flinging off his clothes before making to sleep. But there were further of the guard pressing in at the door, and they were armed with swords.

Little John suddenly removed his shoulder from the door, and into the cell stumbled half a dozen steel-capped fellows. For several moments the little stone chamber was over-full of hard-breathing men, and wild shadows danced on its walls. Little John had armed him with the joint stool that stood by the pallet, and Robin Hood had seized a stool from the first man to fall. Gradually the three outlaws got between their assailants and the door. But Much had suffered a thrust in the arm ere he had skipped round to join his captain, and Little John was grunting as he wielded his uncouth weapon.

'Get free,' cried Robin Hood warningly, and held off three of the enemy with sword-play from the steps, while Much and Little John backed through the door.

Suddenly, without a look behind him, Robin Hood had joined them in the passage, and slammed the door in the faces of the men charging up towards him.

'Lock up fast,' commanded Robin, and Little John put his shoulder to the door again, while Robin sent the bolts on it home, and Much again used his keys.

All the men on duty that night in the dungeon keep were now either exploring the secret passage or cursing one another in the darkness of Robin Hood's cell. The three outlaws found the Guard Room empty except for scattered arms.

'How shall we win out of here, captain?' asked Little John, as Robin Hood fitted on an old-fashioned flat-crowned helmet that covered his head and all his features.

'I shall go out, as I came in, by the Great Entrance,' answered Robin's quiet voice. 'After ten days in this place, do you think it has any secrets from me? Arm yourselves, soldiers of the King, and fall in behind me to chase Robin Hood.'

And as he said, so things befell, and they passed out of the castle by its fine new-built Great Entrance flanked by two drum-towers. They marched out together with a score of men ordered to raise the Town Guard and warn all the warders at the gates. All who met them took them for some of the strange soldiers summoned that day from Wakefield and Pomfret to swell the garrison. So did the warder at the Chapel Bar.

In Nottingham the Town Bell rang all morning, and armed men searched street, alley, and chamber, for Robin Hood. Many citizens searched too, for the Sheriff had offered a goodly reward to any one who should bring back to him his missing prisoner.

But in Sherwood Robin Hood stood as light as a leaf on a tree, by his trysting well, near Beauvale Priory, with his horn at his lips. He blew the three blasts that would tell his band that their captain was come home again, and presently the figures of green men came leaping towards the well from every direction.

Little John turned to Robin Hood and spoke gruffly. He said: 'Captain, now you are safe again, I will say Good-day!' And he stretched out his great hand as if in farewell.

'Nay, by my troth!' said Robin, looking him full in the face. 'This shall not be. If ever you had any love for me, wait awhile to take your leave of a bad master.'

So Little John waited until half a hundred men were gathered about them. Then Robin Hood addressed himself to his band.

'My merry men,' said he, 'I am safe home, thanks to Little John and to Much, who has suffered a wound in bringing me off. Little John has done me a good turn for an ill one I did him. Therefore, henceforth I will be a good servant to him, and he shall be master of all my men and me.'

But at that Little John gave a howl and flung himself on his knees.

'Nay, by my troth,' cried he, 'this shall not be. If ever you had any love for me, take me back to be your fellow, good captain. For master of your men I never can nor will be.'

All the outlaws cheered the sight of a captain who was large-hearted enough to confess himself in the wrong when he thought he had been so, and a fellow who knew how to accept a handsome apology handsomely. Then they banqueted off venison and ale in Sherwood until dusk fell, under green leaves that were still spring-tide small.

PART THREE

ROBIN HOOD & HIS MERRY MEN

AFTER he had been rescued by Little John and Much from Nottingham Castle, Robin Hood spent a jocund midsummer in Barnesdale. He moved up there, out of consideration, he explained, for the Sheriff of Nottingham, who sat shaking in fear of the King's fury when His Grace heard that Robin Hood had escaped.

Many people thought that the Sheriff would at least be deposed from his office. His worst ill-wishers cheerfully prophesied that he would be hanged for neglect of duty. But weeks passed, and no awful judgment arrived from Westminster. At length it appeared that the King was not going to take any action. He had been in high anger when he had discovered that the two strapping men from the North, whom he had appointed Yeomen of the Crown, had been in reality a couple of Robin Hood's followers. He had learnt Little John's nickname, and said: 'This Little John, it seemeth, hath beguiled both the Sheriff and me!' When he was asked what punishment should be inflicted upon the Sheriff: 'Nay,' said he, 'how can I hang up a man for being beguiled, when I was myself beguiled?' It was suggested to him that he should take vengeance on Little John, an expensive suggestion, for the outlaw was safe in Sherwood. A large force would have to be sent to capture him, and His Grace was already distracted by his Welsh wars. He passed from high anger to huge melancholy, as was his custom, and sat with his cheek in his hand, rolling large and sad eyes at the bloodthirsty counsellors sitting around him.

'This Little John is true to his master. I say, by sweet St. John, Robin Hood is better served than the

King of England,' said he.   He pushed away the documents awaiting his signature, and said: 'Speak we no
more of this matter.   Little John hath beguiled us all.'

The outlaws were almost as much disappointed as
the Sheriff's worst enemies to hear such a story of a king.

'Can this tale be true?' asked Will Scarlet of Much.

'I think it very like,' said Much darkly.   He had been
little impressed by his glimpse of the south, although the
King, he said, was of truly royal aspect.

'What was he like?' asked Alan a Dale.

'Very tall, and as well built as any man in his realm,'
said Much, 'with a clear grey eye and glistering gold
hair.   I know my knees shook when I was ushered in to
him.'

'And what business was His Grace about when you
were brought to him?' inquired Will.

'Marry,' said Much, 'he was lying upon a banky of
silk cushions, listening to two ladies of his court singing
ballads to him.'

'At what hour was this?' said Hard-hitting Brand.

'Three of the clock on a fine spring afternoon,' admitted
Much.

'Give me the old King,' grinned Brand.   'The Dean
of St. Paul's fell dead from fright in his presence.'

They were sitting cross-legged in a circle, high up on
Barnesdale, dressed as shepherds.   Some lean upland
sheep were cropping the turf near by, and when Robin
Hood joined them, he too wore a shepherd's long coat
of undyed fleece, and pipes hanging round his neck from
a leathern thong.   He seated himself on a hillock, and
played a few notes before he said: 'Come, light me a fire,
here close by the highway, for I have slain a good fat deer,
and we are to have a great guest to dine with us to-day.'

When they had kindled a lively fire, and set the venison to roast above it, Will Scarlet asked: 'What great one is this comes to dine with us, captain?'

'The Bishop of Hereford rides south from Pomfret this day,' answered Robin, and began to pipe again, a stately measure.

The first spearmen of the Bishop's procession showed on the skyline about noon.   The day was very warm, and in the heat haze dancing above the moorland, their spearheads seemed to quiver.   The Bishop rode attended by a score of soldiers, besides many priests on mules, and it was a comely sight to see so much flashing steel and fine scarlet cloth and embroidery of gold thread, against so blue a sky, into which larks were mounting. The smoke of the outlaws' fire went straight up, and was visible a long way off, but the travellers soon saw that only six shepherds sat around it.   They came on without hesitation.

The Bishop drew rein when he smelt the savoury smell of roast venison, and snapped his fingers at Robin Hood to call him to his saddle-bow.   Adam of Orlton was a crafty-looking Bishop, with many lines made by deep thought in his long pale face.   He asked sternly:

'What matter is this, and for whom do you dress this feast, shepherd?'   His eyes swept the figures of the five smutch-faced outlaws, tending their cookery.   'You are few,' said he, 'to take your King's venison.'

Robin answered him sweetly: 'Lord Bishop, we are poor shepherds who keep sheep all the year.   To-day we are disposed to be merry and have one of the King's fat deer.'

'Your comely King shall hear of your merriment,' said the Bishop, and beckoned a plump of his spearmen.

'Call up your fellows and fall in behind me,' said he to Robin. 'I am going to take you to your King.'

'Lord Bishop!' cried Robin. 'Show some mercy. It ill beseems your lordship's coat to take away so many lives.'

'Why should I show you mercy?' said the Bishop. 'I have caught you red-handed. You are the coolest rogue I ever saw.'

Robin set his back against a thorn, and pulled from beneath his shepherd's coat, his bugle-horn. He set the little end to his mouth and blew a sharp blast. Out of the shaw on the further side of the highway came running three score and ten of his men, led by Little John.

It was indeed a comely sight to see so many strapping men in fine green cloth bowing to their master and his guest under so cloudless a sky.

'What's the matter, captain, that you blow so hastily?' cried Little John.

'The matter,' said Robin, 'is that here I have the Bishop of Hereford, and he cannot find it in his heart to pardon me for taking the King's venison. So I ask myself what shall I do.'

'Cut off his head,' suggested Little John briskly, 'and we will carve you a quiet grave for him up here.'

At that the Bishop's guard, outnumbered and encircled as they were, couched their spears, and Robin Hood's men drew their bowstrings.

'No bloodshed!' cried the Bishop, rising in his stirrups. 'I say I will have no bloodshed.'

'Will you not, indeed?' said Robin Hood, looking at him with interest. 'By my troth, you are the coolest priest ever I met.'

'Humph!' said the Bishop, returning Robin's look. 'I see now I must be the one to ask for mercy. Truly if I had known earlier who you were I should have gone some other way.'

'Into the greenwood,' said Robin Hood, 'to dine you must go.'

'Be it so,' said the Bishop, dismounting. 'I am a man of peace, and hungry.'

The Bishop dismounted from his steed, and Robin Hood gave him his hand, and led him like a bride to the forest lodge where nine months before the outlaws had feasted Sir Richard at the Lee. Will Scarlet with a row of archers waited by the shaw-side with the Bishop's train. 'And be sure that if any man of you seeks to flee,' said he, 'your master gets a dagger in his ribs.'

They had the King's venison for their dinner, but they had also a weary wait, for the Bishop was a prince of trenchermen, and down at the forest lodge he drank wine, ale, and beer as they were offered to him, and discoursed knowledgeably with his host of greyhounds, horses, and hunting, all of which he loved. When he had eaten and drunk his fill, he said:

'Good host, call in the reckoning, for methinks it must be growing wondrous big.'

'Lend me your purse, Bishop,' said Little John, 'and I will let you know what is the cost of this feast to you.'

'I call you to witness that I part with it unwillingly as ever man did,' said the Bishop. 'But as I have said, I will have no bloodshed.'

Little John took the Bishop's purple cloak and spread it on the ground, and told out on to it, from the Bishop's portmantua, three hundred pounds.

'We are much beholden to your lordship,' said Robin Hood. 'Now we will bid you good night, if indeed you will not stay to sleep with us.'

'Now I vow and protest,' said Little John, 'it would be a shame if so great a priest should leave us poor outlaws without holding a service for us. Bethink you, Bishop, how few chances we poor outlaws have for seemly worship.'

So it befell that the Bishop of Hereford held a service in the heart of Barnesdale for Robin Hood and his yeomanry, and after it was brought back in safety to his train at the roadside, with music. And they tell that the Bishop danced in his violet boots to the music made by Robin Hood's minstrels before he turned back to take up his solemn duties and his plots against his King. For, although highly unscrupulous, he was the most prudent of men.

And he left behind him three thoughtful outlaws, for as he mounted his steed he looked long at Will Scarlet, who was holding the fine beast, and said: 'Surely, good squire, we have met before.' Will, who stood a stout six feet, gave him look for look, and answered quietly: 'Never, my lord,' whereupon the Bishop, as if changing the subject, mentioned to Robin Hood: 'I have a long journey this night. For the lord who holds Maxfield for one of the King's wards has given me a tryst.'

He then blessed the three who listened to his words, and putting spurs to his horse cantered forward to join his train. (As a priest he should have been riding a mule, but he was a gentleman that loved to hunt with the hounds, and his stables were never empty of fleet and mettled steeds.) After he was gone Robin Hood, Will Scarlet, and Little John stood watching until the last of his followers were out of sight. They stood in silence, each with his arms folded on his breast, and the eyes of each looked as if he was travelling far in thought. Indeed, all three were looking back eleven years.

ON a day at the end of November, eleven years before
he entertained the Bishop of Hereford, Little John found
himself alone with Robin Hood, in country which he did
not know.   They were travelling north from Barnesdale,
and had left the greenwood for the season.   The floods
were out, and all day they had been picking their way
between mere and marsh.   Although days were short,
the weather had not yet turned cold, and when Robin
said that they might have to lie out this night, but they
must lie dry, Little John merely nodded.

Towards sunset they came upon signs that a house
was near by, and a house of size, and Little John realized
that his master knew well where they were.   When they
struck a path, which presently branched, Little John
would have taken the wider of the two ways, but Robin
said: 'We will approach the house from behind—as
outlaws should.'   And he sighed.   Little John fell in
behind him, and Robin led through several yards, and
past a hog-sty, and around a sheep-fold, no man saying
them nay, for no man saw them.   In the last yard, a
hound barked fiercely at them, but he was chained to his
kennel.   Little John looked at Robin Hood, but Robin
answered: 'No matter.   About this hour the lady of
this place should be coming in from her ride.'   And,
sure enough, a few moments later, when they came in
sideways-view of the house, they heard the barking of
many more dogs, and heard also the sound of horses'
hooves.   Robin Hood helped Little John up into the
branches of a mighty yew (the tree in which to hide in the
winter, for she always wears her greenery), and when

Little John saw the dwelling sideways and beneath them, he admired it so much that he nearly fell out of the tree. It was built of wattle and timber, but it had five gables, and many windows, filled with little panes which reflected the light of the setting sun.   There was a wood of oaks behind it, and a wide noble road leading up to its doors. Down the avenue towards it, was riding a small company —a lady on a mule, two little girls with fox-red curled heads, and a boy on a pony.   They were followed by half a dozen retainers, and by the lady's side, also on a mule, rode a stout pasty-faced man, who smiled as he talked to her.   Much later that night, as they lay on clean straw, in a barn belonging to a merry miller, some five miles further north, Robin woke Little John with a cry of 'Four lives!' 'That's less than half a cat's,' said Little John. 'Whose are they, master?' 'Four lives lie between the false steward of Maxfield and his desire,' muttered Robin, and fell asleep again.   So then Little John knew that the house they had seen was known as Maxfield, and that Robin, as he had guessed, had once known that house well.

During the winter that followed, Little John made it his business to find out a little more of Maxfield, and who dwelt there.   On their way south, with spring, he went near the place again, and picked up a little information, but in the end the person from whom he heard the full story was a tanner of Nottingham town, one Arthur a Bland, kin to him by the mother's side.   Arthur told him, what he had learnt already, that the Lord of Maxfield was missing from home.   He had gone on an embassy from the King to the Prince of Aragon, two years past, and his lady had heard from him that his mission was done, and that he was on his way home, but had heard no more. Some people thought that he must have died of fever. The more gloomy pointed out that in that case some of his retainers should have come back to tell the tale. Nothing had been heard of him since he set sail. Either the ship must have been lost at sea, with all on board, or pirates must have captured her. Meanwhile the lady ailed, and Master Steward ruled. When he heard that one of the two daughters of the house—a little maid, not fifteen years—was likely to become a novice, at Kirklees Priory, Little John thought it best that he should pass by Maxfield again. He told Robin what he knew and what he was going to do, and Robin said: 'It is a pity you are a fellow so easily recognized. I had thought of taking Much.' 'I shall go after dark, and get speech with Young Gamwell,' said Little John— for he had found out that the heir of the house was called Gamwell, and that he was a lad of promise, always at odds with Master Steward.

The month was May, so the trees were bright green, and Little John, in his Lincoln green suit, hung about the house on a moonfull night until he heard all go to bed. He had found out in what room Young Gamwell lay o'nights, and he had noticed that a helpful oak-tree hung a branch close to the leads below its window. When he had squeezed in—for the window was small—he said: 'Whist!' and 'Be not afraid, young master,' for he saw that his coming had woken the lad.

Young Gamwell sat up in his bed, hugging his knees. His eyes were bright and he looked very little afraid, but Little John noticed that on the joint stool beside his pallet lay a small dagger. The boy said, in a whisper: 'Oh! do you come from Robin Hood? I think that you cannot be Robin Hood, for I never heard that he was so tall.'

'I come from him,' answered Little John, and told his name, whereat the boy's eyes grew brighter still, and he said: 'I should like to go with you to him.'

'What, my young master,' said Little John, 'would

Young Gamwell sat up in his bed, hugging his knees

you be one of Robin Hood's men—leave thy horse behind and learn thee to run?'

'He has bidden me not,' said the boy dolefully. 'He has sent me word—or it may have been himself that spoke the word, I do not know—that I must stay here with my mother and sisters.'

'And how do they?' asked Little John.

'I do not know,' said the boy helplessly, 'for my mother lies sick, and weeps always when I visit her. And now my younger sister has fallen sick too. And my elder sister is to go to Kirklees on Lady Day.'

'Must she so?' asked Little John.

'Oh! she wants to go,' explained the boy. 'All her life she has wanted to be a holy nun. But when she is gone there will be only three of us left, and two of them sick.'

'Arr!' said Little John, which was the noise he made when he was thinking. At the end of his thought he said: 'Well, my young master, if Robin Hood has sent you word before that you must stay here, stay you must, for the present. But if aught should crop up that you do not fancy—can you remember the name of Arthur a Bland?'

'The tanner from Nottingham?' said the boy. 'Oh yes, I mind him very well. He comes here often, though not so often as in my father's time. Is he too one of Robin's men?'

That made Little John laugh, and he answered: 'Little Arthur one of Robin's men! Nah! forsooth. He dwells softly, and plies his trade. Not but that he is an honest man, and with a wonderful ear for the news of the countryside. A word to Arthur will always bring me, little master. So until then, God be with you.' Before he swung his long legs out of the window again, he thought to ask, for his own satisfaction: 'What do you know of Robin Hood? You that are so young.' 'I shall be fourteen on Michaelmas Day,' said the boy, sitting up very straight. 'And I am too long for any of my clothes, and can get no new ones.' He held up his right hand, and repeated as if it was a lesson, in a chanting voice: 'Robin Hood lives by the King's deer (though he loves no man in the world so much as his King) and by levies on the evil rich which he distributes amongst the worthy poor. And he will not hear of a wrong thing done without seeking to redress it. And he dwells merrily in the greenwood with seven score men.' He ended sadly: 'And I would go to him. All my life I have wanted to be one of Robin's men—ever since my mother told me of him in secret.'

Little John, who had now heard enough for many hours' thought, merely nodded, and with the words: 'Never fear, some day thou shalt come with me, to the greenwood, through mire, moss, and fen,' he dropped out of the window again.

A month later he heard in Nottingham market that the lady of Maxfield was dead and buried. He could not tell whether Robin knew, for his master had vanished awhile, as was often his custom. The steward at Max-field (said Arthur a Bland) gave out that the lady had died of pure displeasure for the loss of her lord, who was surely also dead, but gossip in Scathelock, the nearest village to the house, was ugly.

Arthur had been to Maxfield, and he had seen young Gamwell, but received no message from him. He had even gone so far—in an undertone, at the funeral feast— as to ask if the young master had any word for his kinsman. Young Gamwell had started, and looked very white, but his answer had been: 'I must wait here.' He had walked away, with a very straight back.

'That's a good lad!' cried Little John.

At the end of a fortnight (Robin having returned),

Little John lay, by his master's side, on the fringe of the forest. They were as green as the young grass beneath them, and they lay with their hats tilted over their eyes, and their hands in their pockets; for every follower of Robin learnt early that it is useless to dress in Lincoln green and hide in a greenwood if you leave face or hands exposed. (Though you deem them brown as a berry, to the eye of one looking for a man, they shine pink as a daisy.) It was a relief to Little John when Robin stirred, and asked: 'What's the time of day?' ''Tis in the prime,' said Little John, blinking at the sun. 'Why then,' said Robin, rising and stretching himself, 'we will to the green-wood gang, for we have no vittles on which to dine.'

It was in the middle of a long green ride that they became aware of a deft young man, shifting fast ahead of them, in the dappled sun and shade. He wore a sad black doublet, and hose which shone like silk, and presently Robin put a hand on Little John's shoulder, to stay him. A herd of deer was in the bend, just ahead of the young man, feeding delicately like ladies, and all unaware. The stranger did not hesitate. He had a bow in his hand. Although he was forty good yards from the deer, he chose the best buck in the herd and found him with his first arrow. Robin Hood ran forward, shouting: 'Well shot!' and Little John, who knew what a hand on his shoulder betokened, slipped behind a tree. But before he hid himself he had seen the stranger turn, and seen that what he had thought a young man was merely a tall boy, looking the taller and older because his raiment was all black. Young Gamwell looked pale when he saw a stranger, who might prove to be a keeper of the King's deer, running towards him; but he did not run away. He stood his ground and shouted, as manly as he would: 'If you come any closer, I'll give you buffets!'

Robin Hood halted and looked young Gamwell up and down. He was a boy with a fall of mouse-coloured hair, and wary grey eyes, frail, but finely made. At the end of his inspection Robin said softly, with a smile which his men knew well: 'Thou had'st best not buffet me!' He drew up his horn, and explained, still smiling: 'Though I may seem forlorn, young sir, yet I have those who will take my part, if I blow this horn.'

'If you blow that horn,' said young Gamwell, 'I can draw a good broadsword, and quickly cut the blast.'

The answer of Robin was to step back a pace and draw his bow. Young Gamwell took his hand from his sword, and drawing his bow, showed himself equally ready to shoot. At that Robin burst out laughing. 'Oh! hold thy hand, hold thy hand,' said he. He explained with great solemnity, 'I think, young sir, that for us to shoot at one another would be a vain thing. For it might befall that one of us twain be hurt. But, if you do greatly desire to slay me, then let us take our swords and bucklers, and have a set-to under yonder tree.'

The tree at which he pointed was that behind which Little John had slipped into hiding, and by the side of it lay a pleasant pond, covered with green slime and flowering weeds. Young Gamwell walked stiffly beside Robin to the place, and said, swallowing hard, as he rolled up his sleeve and tried his blade: 'As I hope to be saved, I shall not give one foot of ground.'

Robin's first blow clearly scared the boy almost out of his wits, but he shouted loudly: 'Never blow shall be better quit.' He raised his sword, brought it down with all his might, lost his footing on the slippery edge of the

pond, and fell backwards.   When he heard a splash, and
a roar, Little John thought that the moment had come
for him to reappear.   The roar had come from Robin,
who was standing, dashing the blood out of his eyes as he
stared at the green-covered sheet of water which seemed
to have swallowed up his antagonist.   Young Gamwell,
as he slipped, had brought down his blade, not upon
Robin's buckler but upon Robin's pate.

The prince of outlaws said, in answer to his merry
man's anxious question: 'I reckoned that pond not above
waist deep, even after rains,' and sure enough, as he spoke,
the head and shoulders of the boy emerged, looking sadly.
Little John, since his master would have none of his help,
and had gone down to the water's edge to bathe his brow,
made a hollow of his hands and shouted in his deepest
tones: 'Yoong maaster, coom oot o' thaat poond.'   He
spoke country-broad, because he was agitated.   The
boy called back: 'I can't.   I've lost my sword.   And I
don't know that it's mine.'   'Oh! go in and find his
sword,' grunted Robin, dashing water over his head, and
feeling his left eye ruefully.   So Little John, making a
slow business of it, took off his hose and shoon and advanced into the green pond, and between them, he and
the boy found the sword, and they waded ashore, to
where Robin was sitting.   Little John sat down too,
and began to put on his hose and shoon, but Young
Gamwell, breathing fast, and shivering, did nothing.
'God a mercy, good fellow,' said Robin presently, 'don't
stand there staring.   Bind up this brow.'   He added:
'I can't see you for honest blood.'   Young Gamwell,
hearing himself called a good fellow, did as he bid,
though not very neatly, and when he had finished,
Robin rose, and said: 'Now, good fellow, tell me who thou

art and where thou dost woon.' The boy answered:
'I was born and bred in Maxfield. My name is Young
Gamwell,' and Robin started, and put a hand to his
bandaged brow. 'I do hope you won't be blind of an eye
hereafter,' said the boy, apologetically. 'You see, I
slipped.' 'You did very well, and I have had a broken
crown before; though not for many years,' said Robin.
'Tell me now, what has brought you to hide in an English
wood?'

'I killed a man,' explained the boy.

At that, Little John gave back a yard, smiting his thigh,
and uttering a sound of despair, but Robin, looking at the
figure before him, who was giving back his look straightly,
asked in level tones: 'Who was this man? What had he
done?'

'He was my father's steward,' said the boy. 'My mother
died, and then I found him forcing my little sister to drink a
potion from a cup. She had been sick, and he had her
on her knee, in an upper chamber, and was telling her
that this would end her pains.' Either from cold, or
some memory, the boy shook in his shoes as he told this
part of his story. 'And did you make him drink of his
own draught?' suggested Robin. 'No,' said the boy,
'I never thought. I just shouted to my sister to beware,
and rushed at him with my dagger. I did remember to
tell him to defend himself, though. And had to back
away to the door, to see that he didn't escape.'

'And how did you escape?' asked Robin.

'He fell over the cup,' said the boy. 'It had got among
the rushes. Every drop in it had been spilt. So now we
shall never know,' he ended, sounding desperate. 'So
now we shall never know,' repeated Robin. 'He was
calling to every one in the house to come up and bind me,

because I had gone mad,' said the boy. 'But we were in an upper chamber. Nobody heard.' 'He caught his foot, and fell on to your blade,' said Robin, sounding as if he quoted. 'Yes,' said the boy.

'And what will you do in an English wood?' wondered Robin after a long silence.

'I am seeking for an uncle of mine. Some call him Robin Hood,' said the boy, sounding less sure.

'Well, then we had best get you a new suit, for you are lacking one,' said Robin, beginning to walk towards the place where the buck had dropped amongst the fern. 'And with your suit of Lincoln green, my sister's son, you must also put on a new name—as I did.'

'Oh!' breathed the boy. 'I wondered . . .'

'And you will never wonder aloud,' mentioned Robin, dropping on his knees to bind the buck for carriage. 'Or call me "uncle."'

'I had thought of calling myself Scathelock,' suggested the boy. 'It is the name of the nearest village to where I was born.'

'And by that token a very bad name for you to choose,' muttered Little John, who was always gruff when he was either touched or hungry.

But when they got into the heart of the forest, carrying the buck between them slung on Little John's long staff, they were jolly enough, singing in chorus:

'And we'll be three of the bravest outlaws
That is in the North Countree.'

The other outlaws, who were waiting for them under the trysting tree, cheered when their master came in sight, bearing so good a dinner, and Robin was careful to say that the bold yeoman who had joined them that noon could bend a good bow.   He snapped his fingers, as if he had forgotten something, while he told them his new man's name, and, clapping his hand to his bandage, brought away a bright stain, after which he announced briskly: 'Scarlet!   His name is Will Scarlet.'

But, in the course of the eleven years that followed, as he grew tall, and stout and broad—and came to speak broad too — Will Scarlet sometimes called himself 'Scathelock.'

IT was autumn again, and a year from the day on which
Robin Hood had lent Sir Richard at the Lee four hundred
pounds. The hart and the hind were getting their
winter coats of brownish-grey. Robin Hood sat at a
table in front of his forest lodge with Friar Tuck, who
was busy with pen and inkhorn and piles of silver pennies.
They were casting up their accounts for the past season,
and setting aside ten marks a head for every member of
the band—pay for the three months of winter during
which their captain would not be amongst them.

The Friar ceased to write, and said, looking up piteously at
the bright heavens above: 'Both the sun and my stomach
tell me that it is three hours past dinner-time, Robin.'

'They tell truth,' said Robin. 'But to-day we expect
a guest to dine with us. I begin to fear that Our Lady
is wrath with me, and I am not to get my loan, given in
her name.'

Little John, who was watching them, said: 'Though
it is three hours past dinner-time, yet the sun is not at
rest. Half of to-day is to come. Still I fear some mishap
may have befallen our knight on his road, for I would
swear he is a true one.'

'You are right,' said Robin. 'Take your bow and tell
Much and Scathelock to wend with you. Get up to the
Sayles and on to the Roman road at the spot where ye
first met the knight. He may have thought that he was
to tryst with us where he did last year. He may have
sent some messenger. Whoever you meet, bring him
down here to dine. For I am weary of counting silver
pennies while you blow down my neck.'

Little John set off obediently, but as well as his long

bow he took a good sword, which he belted on under his vast green mantle.   He hailed Much and Will Scarlet,

It was autumn again . . . the hart and the hind were getting their winter coats of brownish-grey

and they set out together, past the Sayles, which was a small tenancy of the manor of Pomfret, and up on to the Roman road. Here they propped themselves against their accustomed tree and looked out, north towards

Pomfret, west towards Wakefield, and east over level lands vexed by few inhabitants.

Much, who was the one looking north, announced at length: 'Our guest comes—but alas! not the good knight.'

'A Black Monk on a good palfrey,' commented Will Scarlet, following Much's gaze. 'Has sumpter mules with him. Mayhap he has brought our master his pay.'

'Seven sumpters and full fifty men to guard them,' commented Little John. 'I am glad I brought my sword. However, most of the men seem to be kirtled. God grant they wear women's hearts too. For I dare not go back to Robin and tell him the only guest we saw was too largely attended for our liking. Couch down among the mosses now, and be prepared to shoot. But leave the monk that leads this party to me, for I think that he and I be old foes.'

The three outlaws flung themselves down amongst hillocks of the moorland, and not until the monk leading the procession was alongside their hiding-place did Much and Will Scarlet each loose off an arrow into the air, while Little John sprang menacingly into the centre of the road. He seized the monk's palfrey by the bridle, causing it to rear, and shouted as truculently as if he had a hundred men behind him instead of but two:

'Abide, churl monk! Strive to stir an inch, and you and all your men are dead men. And ill luck to you anyway,' he added, 'for you have made my master fast three hours, wherefore he is wrath.'

'And who may your master be, rude knave?' puffed the monk indignantly.

'Robin Hood!' answered Little John in his great voice.

'I never heard any good of him,' said the monk under his breath.

Neither, it seemed, had his train, for as Little John cried: 'Thou liest!' and Much let fly another couple of arrows, the procession broke and scattered.   The monk's guardians fled as fast as they might, back in the direction whence they had come.   They howled the name of Robin Hood and bumped into one another in their haste. Much and Will Scarlet sent a few more arrows down the road amongst them, and they vanished over the skyline uttering faintly that they had fallen into an ambush.   Of all the two-and-fifty followers that the monk had brought with him, only two stayed their ground.   They were a groom and a little page in charge of some of the sumpter mules.

'Come on,' called Little John to them.   'Your master is going to dine with a yeoman of the forest.'

The sun was low in the heavens when the monk and his two attendants, led by Little John and escorted by Much and Will Scarlet, reached the lodge, where dinner was smoking on the table.   When Robin Hood saw his guests, he put off his hood courteously, but the monk's only reply was to pull his cowl further forward.

'I have brought you a churl, captain, as you can see,' said Little John.

Robin Hood, smiling at the round-eyed page, struggling with two heavily laden mules, asked: 'How many men had this guest of ours with him, John, when you met him? Methinks the two he brings here have too many mules to oversee.'

Little John answered merrily: 'He came down the road with two-and-fifty men, captain, but most of them could not stand the sound of your name.'

'Let us blow a horn then,' said Robin, 'that we may entertain with some company a guest that is accustomed to large attendance.'

He set his bugle to his lips, and seven score yeomen, wearing their autumn suits of russet, with mantles of scarlet, striped brown, came pricking out of the brilliant woods.

The monk was offered sweet-smelling water in a silver basin, and fine napery on which to wipe his fingers. Robin led him to sit between himself and Little John, saying: 'Do gladly, strange guest.'

The monk muttered in answer: '*Gramerci*, sir,' but his eyes were at work marking the rich dishes being brought up to the table, and his host had to put his next question twice.

'What is your Abbey, when you are at home, and who is your patron?'

'Eh?' said the monk. 'My Abbey?' Some complacency returned to his face as he announced: 'I am of St. Mary's Abbey at York, and though I am simple here, when I am at home I am High Cellarer.'

'You are,' said Robin, 'the more welcome,' and he called over his shoulder for some of the best wine. 'For now,' said he, 'is my mind at rest. All this day I have been dreading that Our Lady is wrath with me. I was expecting,' he explained, 'some money that was borrowed by a poor knight from me, on behalf of your very Abbey. Now I see that Our Lady has sent me my pay, though not by the man I looked for.'

At that the monk swore with a round oath that never had he heard of any sum borrowed for his Abbey by a poor knight.

'I must not doubt you,' said Robin, 'but what bring you to me on those mules then?'

'Sir,' said the monk, 'twenty marks, no more.'

'No more,' echoed Robin. 'Little John, pray go

examine our guest's mail. If he has indeed no more than twenty marks in all those coffers, we must lend him something for charity.'

'I travel with empty coffers,' said the monk, with rage and fear in his eyes, 'because I ride now to reckon with the Reeves of some of our distant garths, who have certainly been withholding due moneys from us. On my homeward road my coffers will be fuller.'

'They can scarcely be that,' announced Little John, when he returned from taking his count. He roared gleefully in his black beard as he told his master:

'Captain! The monk was truly Our Lady's messenger, but she had doubled your cast. He has brought you eight hundred pounds!'

Sir Richard at the Lee arrived at the last light of sunset. He came in far other guise than yester-year, for he wore a suit of fine scarlet and white cloth, and carried a lance-gay in his mailed hand. A hundred men in his livery attended him, and directly behind him rode a squire, bearing his master's well-burnished helmet.

When he saw Robin Hood and his men seated at their long table in front of the forest lodge, Sir Richard alighted from his palfrey, gave his lance-gay to his squire, and pushed back his hood from his noble grey head. He advanced holding out both hands, and crying:

'God save thee, Robin Hood, and all this company!'

'Welcome be thou, gentle knight!' replied Robin, leaping over the loaded table with a single bound. 'Right welcome art thou! Hast dined or supped? I know not what to call this meal we take now.'

'By my faith,' answered the knight, 'I am glad to see it, call it what you may, for I have not broken bread

since I left Uttersdale.' His face grew graver as he
added: 'This day has been one of mischances for me.'

'I grieve to hear you say so,' said Robin, leading him
to the table. 'For myself I have fared well.' He seated
himself by his guest's side, and asked: 'What need
drives you to the greenwood again, Sir Richard?'

'Have you forgotten our tryst?' said Sir Richard. 'I
can tell you I have not.'

'Oh! Hast thou thy lands again?' asked Robin
lightly.

'Yes, before God,' answered Sir Richard, 'for which
I thank God and thee. But this very morning, as I
was about to mount my horse, I got passing ill news.
The Abbot of St. Mary's at York, my old enemy, has
sent his Cellarer south to visit the High Justice in London,
and buy pleaders and witnesses to prove that some of
my land should not be mine. He has entrusted the
Cellarer with no less than eight hundred pounds to
expend upon the business. I shall never be able to
match him at that game.'

'Indeed,' nodded Robin, 'I fear you never will.'

Fresh dishes were being brought to the table, and he
filled Sir Richard's cup, saying: 'Here's confusion to all
oppressors.'

The knight drank, and said with his sad smile: 'I knew
you would not blame me for coming so late when you
heard my other cause for delay. My own ill news held
me not from the saddle. I swallowed it and rode off to
keep my tryst, though not in such spirits as I had hoped.
But then I came upon something which did give me
to pause.' He took absently of some doe-pasty. 'It
was in a village called Wentbridge,' he said, 'the first
through which we passed after we had left Pomfret behind

us.   We found ourselves held up by a great press hastening to a wrestling match.   You know the kind of thing,
and how our north-country folk crowd to it.   There were
men, women, children, dogs, and even cats running to see
the show.   The prizes were set out in the little market-
place, and were fair to see—a snow-white bull, a mettlesome courser, saddled and bridled, a pair of gloves, a
red gold ring, and a pipe of wine.   Since I had some
attendance with me more than I generally use, and also
heavy sumpter horses, I might not pass on my way
quickly.   And to tell truth, I did not call to my men to
hurry or push any aside.   Over-eager spectators at a
gathering like this are apt enough to brawl with strangers.
Besides, I had already marked, as ripe for mischief, a
party of soldiers, fellows fresh from the Welsh marches,
judging by their talk.   They wore the livery of that cousin
of our King who always so opposeth His Grace.   They
may have come, like us, from Pomfret, which is that great
lord's chief castle, or from a dark keep which I could espy,
a little to the west, over the waters of Went.   Be that as
it may, they had ranged themselves like guards all around
the ring in which the sport was taking place, and they
shouted continually for a certain Welsh champion, whom,
as I learnt from those about me, they had carried here
with them.   The simple villagers were looking lowering,
as well they might, pushed by late-comers from all the
best places from which to see the show.   They shouted
for a champion of their own parts, one Clym of the
Clough, an upstanding yeoman, with a fell of flax hair
like that of our Much here, hands like hams, and shoulders
almost as broad as those of Scathelock.

'As they waited, chest to chest, each grasping the
other with locked hands round the body, and each with

his chin on the other's right shoulder, I looked from the Yorkshireman to the Welshman, and said to myself that here, by the grace of God, should be a good match. (When I was younger I knew some chips of the sport myself.) For the Welsh Marcher, though smaller and lighter than this Clym, looked a skilful knave. He had the quick black eyes and ragged rusty beard of his race. As he entered the ring he bowed vaingloriously to north, south, east, and west. When I had looked also at the soldiery holding the market square north, south, east, and west, I decided to stay there a little. For I smelt oppression, and though I am no lover of trouble, yet when there is oppression in the air, a knight may not wend his way.

'I soon saw that I was right. The Welshman was to win, or his adherents would know why. At first I thought that he might well win, for very shortly after that worthy of the village whose duty it was had given the signal for them to fall to, the Welshman used a cunning back-heel. Clym had been on the point of lifting him from the ground. He replied with an outside-click. In this he was very wise, for at hypes and hanks, as will appear, he was no match for Clym, a rock of a fellow, that could lightly lift him. At twists and turns, however, the Marcher was the master. He was a very eel of the mud-waters, and with that outside-click all but overset Clym. Indeed,' said Sir Richard, with a light in his faded eye, 'for a little as I watched the sport, I fear I forgot my tryst in Barnesdale which was so dear to me, and the reason why I had stayed on my road. Nevertheless, I was not long allowed to forget my suspicions. The Welshman, still fresh, and much the attacker, tried an outside stroke, striking Clym on the ankle. Clym recovered, shaken,

and answered with a stout breast-stroke, twisting more
featly than you would have credited of a man of his size.
But the Welshman was ready for him. (I can tell you
there was roaring enough by now.) With great cunning
he essayed to end the business with a goodly hank,

Clym had been on the point of lifting him from the ground

turning like lightning and lifting his great adversary clean
off the ground. Clym, no child in arms, fell with him,
but not undermost. Every one could see that. It was
clear as the daylight. The wrestlers had fallen in one and
the same moment, but side by side.'

Sir Richard beat with his dry hand on his knee, after
his custom when he was making a point. 'It was a dog-
fall, if ever there was one, and so the judges decreed it,

and ordered the bout to begin anew. But they could not make themselves heard, so great was the jubilation of the Welshman's supporters, crying aloud that the match was over and he was the victor, having brought Clym of the Clough to the ground undermost.

'At that,' said Sir Richard, 'I gathered my reins, and moved forwards into the press, crying as loud as I might: "A dog-fall! A dog-fall!" The judges, who were poor simple folk, and had been beginning to look wan, plucked up spirit to echo my cry. The soldiers, for their part, at first tried to shout me down, and one fellow went so far as to shake his fist at me. I knocked his cap over his eyes with the butt of my lance-gay, and by the grace of God he spoke not again. For his companions had looked at me, and had seen that I rode with a hundred men in my livery, whereas of them there were a scant fifty. Also I had the right on my side, which I hope worked in their hearts. Be that as it may, they offered no resistance when I prodded the judges to announce in the sudden silence which had dropped upon that square since my riding forward: "A dog-fall! The bout begins anew!"'

'And that is nigh the end of my tale of the wrestling,' said Sir Richard, 'for in the new bout Clym very shortly performed a perfect swinging hype, and the Welshman was thrown to the ground and there lay, with his victor straddling above him, plain to see. Then the judges cried that Clym of the Clough was the prize-winner, and Clym, smiling like the full moon, bent to offer the Welshman his hand.

'In the same moment what I had dreaded came to pass. The soldiers, forgetting all caution in their grief at the fall of their champion, made to fell Clym. They closed

in around him with raised fists, some twenty of them, and
I lost sight of him.   I couched my lance and drove as
fast as I honestly might towards the spot, much encum-
bered in my passage by shrieking women and flying men.

In the new bout . . . the Welshman was thrown to the ground

Behind me pressed my men, with bows bent.   I gave
them the signal to shoot across the mob, not into it, for
fear of slaying the innocent.   This they did, and since
we were armed with lance-gays and the soldiers had none,
they scattered, leaving Clym to us.   Then I was happier,
though not yet easy.   I stood up in my stirrups and

shouted: "Clym of the Clough wins!" while some of my men knocked down with the butts of their lance-gays such of the soldiers as were still combative. By the grace of God that settled the matter. The soldiers, seeing that they could not take vengeance on Clym, paused for thought. I have heard that their lord is ready with his gallows, and certainly no lord ever desires that his garrisons shall fall into feuds on holidays, slaying folk in his villages. Also the Welshman, an honest fellow as so good a wrestler should be, had arisen, unhurt, and was crying: "Gentlemen! Gentlemen! Indeed it would be a pity for you to slay Clym of the Clough. To-day he has thrown me, but we may meet another day."

'One of the soldiers, determined to make the best of a bad affair, then came up to me and said: "Your pardon, sir knight. Had we known the Yorkshireman was your man, we would have granted his victory gladly." Which,' said Sir Richard, beating his hand up and down again, 'was the wrong reason for doing the right thing, as I presently had to show him.

'After I had done that, I gave Clym five marks to buy wine for all his friends, and I left him, serving bumpers to the Welsh champion and several of his supporters. They were like hounds that have fought in kennel—a few torn ears and closed eyes to show, but no malice left and much shame. I deemed it safe enough to leave them and keep my tryst. And although I was sorry that now I must be late, yet for love of Robin Hood I was glad that no poor yeoman had been worsted.'

Sir Richard had ended his tale. Robin Hood said heartily: "'Fore God, sir knight, I thank you in the name of all yeomen for the deed you did to-day. Whoever

helps a good yeoman is my friend.' And he called Alan
a Dale and his band of minstrels to give the guests some
music while they finished their supper. After the board
had been cleared, Sir Richard said to his squire:

'Gamlyn, go bid the grooms bring here the loads from
the sumpters.' So presently there were set upon the
greensward in front of the forest lodge many large leathern
bags and one small one. 'Have here, gentle Robin,'
said Sir Richard, 'the four hundred pounds you lent me.
I have added twenty marks in thanks.'

But at that Robin began to laugh.

'Nay, 'fore God,' said he. 'Your debt has already
been paid to me to-day—and overwell. It would be a
shame for me to take twice. Nevertheless, gentle knight,
you are much the most welcome of the guests that have
dined with me this day.'

'By my troth,' said Sir Richard, 'I do not understand
you. Pray take up your due.'

Robin said softly: 'Our Lady sent me by the Cellarer
of her Abbey at York to-day, eight hundred pounds. I
think that Cellarer will not ride south to see the High
Justice on your affairs now. He spurred homewards a
few minutes before you arrived. I bade him tell his
Abbot to send me such a monk to dinner every day.'

The grooms were still unloading packages—a hundred
bows of the best yew wood, and a hundred arrows, each
nocked with silver, feathered with peacock's wing, and a
full ell long.

Robin said: 'Never did I see so good a store of bows
and bolts. But what do they here?'

'With your will,' said Sir Richard, 'they are a poor
present to you. My son made most of the arrows with
his own hands. He was fain to see you. But it is ill

for an only son to sit at home winding wool for his lady
mother, in his sire's castle. So I have sent him to learn
warfare on the Welsh marches.'

'I like your son's gift better than any ever made to
me,' said Robin. 'Pray tell your knaves to gather up
your money bags while mine take up my bows and arrows.
And since Our Lady sent me twice your debt by the
Cellarer, I have instructed Little John to part it in twain.
Have back thy four hundred pounds and with it another
four hundred. And if at any time you fail for money,
come to Robin Hood. For, 'fore God, while Robin
Hood has any left, it will be at the service of Sir Richard
at the Lee.'

On an April day of spring sunshine and sudden hail-
storms, a most unlikely figure came riding into the greenwood. Robin Hood, Will Scarlet, and Little John, who
had just cooked their breakfast over a small fire at the
forest's edge, looked down, and saw, toiling up the hill
towards them, a lady all alone. There was a rainbow
in the inky clouds above her, her riding suit was all
black, and she was mounted on a coal-black palfrey,
whose black velvet housings swept the grass. They
could not judge of her face, for that was covered by a veil
of the cobweb lawn called Cyprus, after the island from
which such stuffs came. They were not entirely surprised to see the lady so richly dight, for they had heard,
days past, that the King was on his road to York with
his court; but a lady alone, and so attired, was certainly
something strange. Little John made a movement to
stamp out the fire, but Robin stayed him, and standing
up and sweeping off his cap, called out: 'Good morrow,
fair madam!' He bowed low, and she, in the voice of
one accustomed to command, but in a foreign accent,
cried: 'Doant rrun away!' The outlaws waited, cap in
hand, until she was close to them, when Robin said:
'Fair madam, we have no thought of flight. But whence
come you, and where go you, in such mournful plight?'

'I come from Lon-don,' replied the lady, sounding
very tired.

'From London upon the Thames!' exclaimed Little
John.

'I nevare 'ear of any other. And one is quite enough,'
said the lady. Her voice was quite young, but Will

thought he had never heard a lady so rude. 'And I need three champions,' she announced.

'Is London then besieged with foreign arms?' asked Robin softly.

'Not at all,' snapped the lady, 'unless you could call the Prrince of Aragaon and his suite an invasion. Myself, I should. He has brought a suite of a hundred,' she went on briskly, 'and two giants, and nothing will please the Queen, whom I serve, but that these grisly creatures shall be given brides in England.'

'Are they really giants, madam?' asked Little John, drawing himself up.

At that the lady laughed, and admitted: 'I think they are all as tall as you. That is what made me call out to you not to rrun away. But they are said to wear living serpents, hissing on their helms, instead of a plume. And unless three Englishmen can conquer them, they are to be given two of the King of England's wards.'

'English ladies!' gasped Will.

'Myself,' said the lady, 'I am of Champagne, in France; but the other lady is all English, and my dearest friend. We twain sit on the same cushion, sew the same seam, and are like two cherries on one stalk,' she explained prettily. 'And the Queen has sent four of us abroad, to look for English champions — one to the east, one to the west, one to the south, and one to the north. I am the one sent north,' she ended, and threw back her veil.

She was as fair a damsel as ever even Robin had seen, for her eyes and hair were black as her gown and her steed, and her skin was as white as snow. And when she saw that the outlaws thought so, she blushed, although she was a court lady, and looked the fairer.

'Good madam,' said Will, saying straight out what he thought, 'you should not ride alone.'

This made her cry out: 'Bah!' She lifted a silver whistle, which hung round her neck on a silver chain, and blew a shrill blast. At once a boy on a pony came into sight. 'Her Grace has given us each a page in attendance, and two hounds,' she said. 'This is my cousin, leetle Dickee Patrinton. He was sent to my father's castle, by my aunt, to learn good manners, and when my father died, and I became a ward of the Crown, the Queen took him too. He reminded her of an angel.'

Dick Patrinton did look like an angel, for he had floss-silk fair hair, reaching to his shoulders, and pink pin-cushion cheeks, and round innocent blue eyes, and he was dressed in a pale blue-and-white suit, with heart-shaped silver buttons, and lily-white hose. He said: 'I am sorry, but you didn't tell me until we were out of the town that we were going into the green-wood; so I had to go back for my ferret.' And, sure enough, there was a little white fur head, with ruby eyes, peeping out between two of the buttons of his tunic.

'I might have been murdered, but it is no matter,' said the lady, 'for our search is happily at an end. I have found three English champions to fight the Prince and his giants at York.'

'Oh, have you, lady?' asked Little John, guffawing.

'Certainly!' said the lady, turning to Will. 'But when you have won, and the King tells you to claim the victor's prize, you are not to choose my dearest friend, whose name is Joan. For she loves my cousin Jacques, who is Dickee's elder brother, and he loves her. And they were going to fly to France together, only that would have been treason; so he became weak-kneed. But she means to have him.'

She smiled at Robin, and asked: 'Will you adventure life and blood to free two ladies fair?'

'When is the day?' asked Robin. 'Tell me that and no more.'

'Midsummer next,' said the damsel, 'which is June the twenty-four.'

'Say no more, lady,' nodded Robin. 'And that you may know us (for we cannot come into York bare-faced), look on that day for the men who wear pilgrim's gear.'

So thus the affair was happily settled, and the lady became very gracious, and stayed to dine with them, in the forest, and Dick Patrinton was shown by Little John how to bend an outlaw's bow; and the Queen's two hounds (who had been called by her Adam and Perrot, after her greatest friend and her greatest enemy in England) dined well on stewed hare.

During the two months that followed the outlaws practised broadsword-play nightly, and in the second week of June, Robin Hood, Little John, and Will Scarlet set out for York city. They wore doublets and hose of faded grey, that had weathered many a storm, and long grey cloaks that looked motley, for they were patched with brown and black. Each wore by his side a little scroll of parchment and a water-bottle, and carried a long shepherd's crook. Their large flopping black hats were trimmed with shells, and every one who fell in with them on the road took them for pilgrims come from the Holy Land. No one guessed that a covered cart, which Arthur a Bland drove through the city gates a few hours before them, contained, under many piles of hides and pelts, three good swords and shields, and all the disguise

for three strange English champions.   They met Arthur
beneath the city walls, with sunset, and he told them that
the show was fixed for noon, and only two parties of
Englishmen were expected to oppose the Prince of Aragon
and his giants.   One of the parties came from London;
the other was made up of young courtiers, and was not
thought likely to stand stout blows.   Indeed, it was said
in the town that the whole affair was just an excuse by
the Queen for a pageant, to please herself and flatter a
visiting foreign prince.   The giants were black of skin—
Moors, whom the Prince's father had taken in battle and
given to him as slaves.   But they were certainly large,
and might know outlandish tricks in fighting.   (Most
English champions, these days, were busy preparing to
fight the Scots.)   Little John brightened when he heard
that the Moors might be skilful.   His face had fallen as
he thought that he had been lured out of the greenwood
for next to nothing.   The outlaws returned to their inn,
and supped frugally, drinking water only, and went to
bed before Phoebus had sunk behind the Minster towers.
They were given pallet beds in a room under the beams
kept for pilgrims, with holy texts painted on the walls,
and they all slept soundly.

The morning of the contest was very hot, a perfect
Midsummer Day in Old England, and it soon became
clear that although the affair might be only an excuse for
a pageant, the Queen had spent lavishly, and the people
of York were all going.   Arthur a Bland met the outlaws
again, in grey dawn, in an unused forester's hut, in a
small wood outside the town, and there they put off their
motley attire and became English champions—but pilgrims still.   Much and a pedlar called Kit o' Thirsk
were there to help them, and had brought three horses

so handsome that Robin, as he ran his eye over the quarters
of the fairest, pulled his chin and said: 'I hope Bishop
Adam doth not recognize that bargain!' They dressed
themselves in black suits and silver arms, with scallop
shells embroidered on their surcoats, and as they dressed
—looking forth from the hut on to a smooth mere,
adorned with water-lilies—they heard a continual clatter
and chatter coming from the high road above.   Every one,
even from the country outside, was trooping into York
city this Midsummer Day to see two black giants and a
foreign prince fight Englishmen.

At length they were ready, and Robin gave the word,
and hopped into the saddle of his spirited chestnut, which
had once been a bishop's pride.   Will Scarlet had a dapple-
grey steed, and Little John a roan.   They trotted off,
and found that they had done well to start early, for the
roads were blocked, even on this side of the town.   They
had to ride right through, for the ground appointed for the
pageant lay on the north of the Minster, so when they got
to the city gates they pulled down their visors, which made
them very hot.   They were gladly let in when they called
that they had come to fight, and people tried to make room
for them to pass, but they had a long wait behind a
procession of chariots bringing ladies, and as they drew
near the plain they heard shouts which made them fear
that the show was begun.   However, when they arrived
they were told that the shouts had merely meant that the
foreigners had vanquished the London men.   The courtiers were yet to come.   Dick Patrinton must have recognized them from the shells on their breasts, for they
found him, presently, sidling up towards them, pushed
this way and that by townsfolk who were grumbling that
they could not see the King.   This was because the stand,

in which the lordly folk were sitting, had been built so
large and so high that the figures in it looked like dolls.
The outlaws could make out — through their closed
helms—a doll dressed in cloth of gold, with a white head-
dress, whom Dick said was the Queen, and grouped
around her a bank of ladies looking like a bank of flowers
—in gowns of Douai green and rose-scarlet.   The King
had brought the lion which he always carried with him
on his travels, to watch the fighting.   It was chained to
a post beneath the stand, and men with long poles were
beating off small boys who wanted to poke it.   The King
was not sitting by his spouse's side.   He had dined with
his company of Genoese fiddlers, of whom he was very
fond, and was standing amongst them, choosing the
music they were to play.

After a long and weary pause trumpets and kettledrums
sounded, and the Prince of Aragon and his giants rode
into the ground for the second time.   They rode all
around it, bowing and saluting as they passed those
seated in the stand, and Little John was able to satisfy
himself that although the giants were wearing serpents in
their helms, these were not alive.   They were very terrible to look upon, having been cunningly fashioned,
but they were clearly of silvered metal.   The Prince rode
between his giants, who wore floating white draperies
over their armour,   He was nothing to look upon himself, being narrow-shouldered and thin-shanked; but the
horses of all three were truly worshipful.   The fiddlers
struck up, and the band of English courtiers who were to
fight the foreigners next trotted into the ring.   Every one
roared applause, for they were well matched for size,
all tall men, and wore plate armour of the new fashion,
with surcoats sewn with roses and lilies, and helms of the

shape called *bassinets*. They managed their handsome steeds well too—all were heavy bays—but not with the careless ease of the foreigners. Little John, when he had studied them, gave Will a dig, and mentioned—'Over-weighted!'

Half a dozen mounted men-at-arms, with roses and lilies on their surcoats, followed them into the sandy plain. One of them carried a small square flag, wired stiff, and matching their surcoats, and in front of them rose a marshal who carried a baton. This company ranged up on one side of the striped wooden barrier, which ran waist-high right across the lists, and opposite to them appeared half a dozen Aragonese—men of olive complexion, with leopard skins slung above their muslin surcoats and their arms, which were of a dark blue hue, with a design of writhing serpents, suns with rays, birds in flight, and much else.

The crowd gave a heave now, and Dick explained that the damsels who were to be the victors' prizes were to be displayed again. They were mounted on small long-tailed white jennets, and they cantered round the ground, either because they had no reason to fear tiring their steeds or because, as seemed likelier, they were eager to be done with the business. One of them was the French lady who had come to find champions in the greenwood, but the outlaws would scarcely have known her, for she was dressed all in white to-day, and she had her long curling black hair streaming down her back, and, set rather far behind and askew on her head, a small wreath of roses and lilies. The other damsel resembled her in every way except that her tresses were fox-red, and her eyes were grey. They rode with their chins up, looking straight ahead, and some folk in the crowd said 'twas a

shame to give such damsels to Moors, and others thought
that, with so fair a prize, now surely blood should be
spilt.   Little John asked Dick, in his practical way,
sounding shocked: 'Will the King give English lands
with these ladies to the paynims ?'   'I believe,' said Dick,
'that he will not.   It is said that he means to keep their
lands, saying that the gift of the ladies themselves is
sufficient compliment to the Prince.   And the Prince
has promised that the paynims shall be baptized before the
weddings.   But none of this will come to pass, saith my
cousin, whose name is Tiphaïne.'

'And how is the other damsel called?' asked Will,
straining his eyes after her (for he had lifted his visor).

'Oh! she is Joan of Maxfield,' said Dick.

At last the King was seen to ascend his seat, beside the
Queen, but he was so far off that the outlaws could see
nothing except that he wore a long gown of red figured
with leopards on it, and a hat like a pie, only made of
some gold stuff, turned up with white fur and with a
crown *fleury* sitting on the top.   Beneath the royal couple
sat the damsels who had ridden round the lists, looking
like little white dots.   The Genoese fiddlers ceased to saw
their instruments, the trumpets blew, and as the com-
batants rode away from one another, towards the further
ends of the lists, Dick, leaning against Robin Hood's
well-mannered chestnut, said with a grin: 'I have wagered
my ferret that the young Despenser bites the dust this
day.   He cannot ride.'   The perky page had his ferret
up his sleeve, a thing not easily to be discovered, except
by the odour, for Dame Isabeau's choice of a pageant
dress for her pages was a round cloak, fresh from France,
covering a boy from collar to knee, crowded with roses
and lilies embroidered, and the letter 'I' under a crown.

See page 138

A most unlikely figure came riding into the greenwood

The champions' grooms were lifting housings to tighten girths, and the champions, each of whom had received a very long and heavy-looking tilting lance, with a gilded butt, painted red and white for a yard or more, were testing their soundness, and twisting round their sword-belts. 'And what do you get if you win your wager?' asked Robin, to which Dick answered: 'Well, a pound of sweetmeats, in a wooden box, carved with hounds' heads.' He added: 'I laid my wager with the Master Carpenter (who lets me make boats sometimes) and the Master Cook.   Thus, if I lose, my sweet beast shall not starve.'

The trumpets blew again, and the marshal flung up an arm, and the champions charged; the Prince and his giants uttering outlandish cries.   The crowd gave another heave, and when next Will looked down, Dick was gone, and he was surrounded instead by a boys' school, in charge of a master, two women with wide-open mouths, and children wailing somewhere amongst their skirts, and an old gaffer drinking out of a bottle.   In the first encounter, the Prince, one Moor, and two English courtiers broke lances, which snapped as flowers do, not clean across but droopingly, which gave them a foolish look as the riders retired.   When they had charged again Robin said aloud, not knowing the boy had vanished: 'Your sweet beast is safe, Dick,' for two of the courtiers were carried from their saddles by the Moors' spears, and one of them seemed like never to rise again, because of the weight of his new armour.   He lay on his back, beating the air, and rolling to and fro, like a babe in swaddling bands on a nurse's knee.   The other did not stir at all, and the crowd shouted that he had hit his head on the wooden barrier, as he fell, and that he was in Fairyland, for the nonce.   But the one Englishman

left, after both he and the Prince had broken spears, and
been unhorsed, had a worthy set-to on foot, with broadsword and buckler, and it was not until the Englishman's
sword broke off at the hilt that the marshal called an order,
and the trumpets crackled, and the man carrying the
flag with roses and lilies upon it, dipped that until it
touched the sand.

After that there was confusion for a little, and a whistle
sounded, and surgeon's men came running to the assis-
tance of the vanquished. In the end, however, both
walked off the field, though somewhat wavering in gait,
and walking like men upon ice, because of the encum-
brance of their new armour. Next, the King's lion was
brought his dinner, so that the champions hitherto
victorious might rest awhile, and the populace be given
something rare at which to stare. But although the
bones carried in were so many and glorious that the men
bearing the dish seemed to bend under its weight, the
King's lion finished all in a wonderfully short space of
time, and looked around for more. The Prince and his
giants presently mounted fresh horses, and the fiddlers
ceased to play again, and the marshal cried that the last
champions of the day would now enter the field. He
stood up in his stirrups—for he was a little knight—and
asked Robin Hood how he and his followers were called,
and Robin answered through his closed visor: 'We three
be three Old English Pilgrims'; so the marshal announced
that, and the crowd laughed, and thought the show would
soon be done. And in this they were right, but not as
they foresaw.

For there was never so short and certain an encounter
as that of Robin Hood, Little John, and Will Scarlet,
with the Prince of Aragon and his giants.

Robin had always warned his followers that they had faint hope of unhorsing the foreigners, or of excelling them in tilt-yard skill. They must get them a-foot, and trust to sword and buckler. So, after the first charge, in which Little John was unseated, and the Prince's spear was shattered, Robin, casting his spear away, flung himself from his horse, and drew his sword. The Prince, casting away his spear butt, did likewise, and they began to exchange stout blows over the barrier. The two Moors made haste to do as their master, and out of the corner of his eye, as he parried the blows of both, Will saw Little John scrambling to his feet. The steeds of all three, being prepared for such doings, walked quietly aside, as if to watch the fray, looking down their long noses patiently.

Then Little John, with the first blow of his broadsword, felled a Moor to the ground, and in the same moment Will sent the sword of the second spinning into the sand, and meanwhile Robin Hood had cleft the Prince's helm, and brought him to his knee. The marshal, trotting up and down in anxious haste, flung down his baton, and all the trumpets sounded, and whistles blew. In the stand, the King had risen to his feet, calling for 'No more!' and the two foreign ladies were laughing and crying at once. One of the Moors crawled from the scene upon all fours, because of the wounds he had suffered; and without their grisly helms, and with their white garments all stained and disarrayed, truly the Prince of Aragon's giants did not look so awful as they had done when charging on their fleet horses and uttering war-cries. The second of them followed his master up to the King and Queen, but was dismissed by the Prince with a single word: 'Baboon!' whereat he bowed to the sand, and drew back, with eyes rolling, and stood with his arms folded upon his breast. The Prince of Aragon, when he had shed his arms, appeared of a strangely pallid countenance, with lips as thin as string, and the eye of a serpent, but he showed himself very princely in his defeat, which he admitted that he had not at all foreseen. In a flowery speech he told the King and Queen that, nevertheless, he would like to make them the gift which he had prepared for the end of to-day's pageant. He clapped his hands, and a procession of his gentlemen came towards him, escorting a lord well-stricken in years, with a wondering look, and twisted bronzed features, and a double-fork grey beard. 'This lord,' said the Prince, 'was taken at sea, in a pirate ship of Barbary, by some of my seamen, late this season. And I carried him straightly with me, to England, to give back to his King. For he protesteth that he is English, and was once sent upon an embassy to my country, by the late King of England, of warlike memory, whose soul God rest. He hath pulled an oar in the galleys, eleven years.'

The King of England that was now drew back and shook in all his limbs when he heard this speech, as if he had an ague. For although he was of a goodly stature, and strong-limbed, he never loved to hear the name of his warrior sire, or, to tell truth, anything of a fearsome nature, such as battles, galleys, pirates, or dungeons. But his defection was nothing noticed, for even as the Prince spoke, the red-headed damsel who had been appointed to be one of the victors' prizes this day, leapt upon the strange English lord, like a young greyhound, to the cry of: 'Father! Father!' and he, clasping her in his arms, answered: 'Joan! Little Joan!' Joy shone in her face, while tears ran down his furrowed cheeks, and as for the damsel, she danced and twinkled like a star. And whilst the Lord of Maxfield and his orphan child hugged and kissed one another, the lists became full suddenly of people running up to the foot of the stand to see what was toward. Cheers soon rent the air, and also, since the scene was set in England, a sharp shower came on, and the Queen, who was a lady that liked to be the centre of any scene, fell in a swound. While her ladies revived her, the King, who knew her swounds, spoke again, in a comfortable manner, laughing and asking: 'But where be the little Davids that vanquished our Goliaths? They must get their reward.'

(He could not know that, even as he spoke, in a forester's hut, outside the town, Robin Hood and Little John were casting to Much and another of their followers helms and coats adorned with scallop shells, and amidst much laughter were putting on some other disguise. What this was, no song tells, but two weary horses were safe in the greenwood next week.)

Only one English pilgrim was to be found to receive his meed from the King, and that was Will Scarlet. He stood with his helm under his arm, much heated in countenance, and with the air of one who would sooner be elsewhere, blurted out that his fellows seemed to be gone home. He dropped on his knee when he said this, as if he feared it lacked respect, but it made the King laugh, and say: 'I promised two ladies as prizes. You cannot have both.'

Will looked worse when he heard these words, but he was saved further grief by the damsel Joan, who advanced with comely grace, took him by the hand, and called out: 'I will do the choosing!'

The end of this story was made into a song of Robin

Hood, and often sung, in days of old, in garden, great-hall, camp, kitchen, and nursery.

> With that, a noble lord stepped forth,
>   Of Maxfield earl was he,
> Who lookt Will Scathelock in the face,
>   Then wept most bitterly.

> Quoth he, 'I had a son like thee,
>   Whom I loved wondrous well;
> But he is gone, or rather dead.
>   His name was Young Gamwell.'

> Then did Will Scadlock fall on his knees,
>   Cries, 'Father! father! here,
> Here kneels your son, your Young Gamwell,
>   You said you loved so dear.'

But the song does not tell whether Will gave up being an outlaw, and became Young Gamwell again, and returned with his father and sister to Maxfield. Indeed, although he may have done so for a little while, he cannot have stayed long, for his name is to be found in most songs of Robin Hood, and he was certainly with his master at the last.

Also, he did not wed the French lady. She wedded, in the fullness of time, a cousin of her own, of French descent, but a gentleman that had gained, by reason of his singular favour with both King and Queen, his quick wit, and his handsome person, much gold and broad lands in England. He was called Sir Richard Patrinton, and his Dame Tiphaïne on winter evenings and on summer mornings, with the spring tide, and with the fall of the leaf, would often tell her damsels in waiting how their lord had worshipped her from afar, as a holy saint in a

Will Scarlet

niche, since she was a mere babe.   This tale always made
them pull faces behind their embroidery frames, for they
knew her senior, and that the rosemary bushes did not
grow to such magnificence in her garden without reason.
For the saying in Old England has always been that where
rosemary flourishes, there the dame wears the breeks.

THE Scots wars kept the King in the north, much against his will, for the better part of two years after he came to York. Throughout a very wet August, held to his task by his masterful cousin of Lancaster, he laid siege to Berwick, which, much to his shame, had been in Scots hands sixteen months. The Scots ravaged Yorkshire in his wake. His Queen, with their three children, was sent for safety to a place called Brotherton, on the River Aire. There was no town there, only a village, but a very fair country palace, in which a prince called Thomas, step-brother to the present king, had been borne by another French queen, aunt to the present Queen. Also, it lay within a few miles of Lancaster's strong castle of Pomfret.

On the last day of August, Robin Hood and Little John, who commonly wintered together, were making their way north on foot. They had quitted Barnesdale the day before, and had reckoned to sleep that night in Pomfret town, but with a wild dusk they were still some miles distant, and in soft country. With the coming of darkness the wind, which had been driving the rain in their faces all day, ceased, for which they were glad, for the moon was at the full, and presently she began to show herself between ragged clouds, moving fast.

'We must step on,' quoth Robin, 'for here is nothing but marsh. But to step on, we must go north, and already, I fear, we have overshot our mark.'

At the edge of a mere, around which they had been working their way, they came in sight of a shepherd, hurrying his flock towards them. He was urging his dog to hasten the sheep, and when the outlaws hailed him, using the broad accent of Barnesdale, he would not stop. He shouted, above the barking of his dog, and the baa-ing of his tumbling flock, to ask them where they would go, so they answered: 'Stump Cross.' He only shook his head, in token that he knew not the name, and cried back: 'This is Water-Fryston.' As he passed by they saw that his face was pale, although he was so hot with hurry. He flung up a hand and cried: 'The Scots are coming,' before he vanished from their view.

Robin Hood paused, and Little John asked: 'Master, of what do you think?' 'Marry,' said Robin, 'I think that this place is very well named, for seldom was I wetter. But I think too that if it is truth that the Scots are so close, we had best, as they say, gang warily.' 'They are a hundred miles south of what they should be, if that man does speak truth,' reflected Little John.

They pressed on, uphill, in the direction whence the man had come, and before long they saw a red glow on the horizon. Little John, as his master trod towards it with a quickened step, reminded him: 'If the Scots have fired a vill, or a farm, we had best gang warily.' 'If the Scots have fired a vill or a farm,' said Robin, 'two Englishmen may help to put out the flames and succour innocent folk.'

As they drew nearer, and saw through the tree-trunks of an old coppice flames leaping against the cloud-raced night sky, they perceived that the lights were scattered and several, and by no means so large as to mean that even a rick was ablaze. They kept inside the wood until they were on its edge, with a low bank between them and the men above, and then they flung themselves full length, amongst bracken and bramble, and peered over.

There was a great company of strange men between

them and the high road which ran across the moor, and the invaders had evidently camped for the hours of darkness, in some fashion, and were feasting. They had lighted fires, and were roasting whole sheep, slung above them. That the sheep were fresh killed was told by the skins dangling from the branches of a tree overlooking the scene. Little John listened to the strangers' speech, and watched their movements, for a full moment before venturing the opinion, 'Scots, indeed!' Their dress, excepting their footwear, was not unlike that which he often wore himself, when travelling, but they all looked men accustomed to live hard, who had, of late, been living right hard. Of their speech he could not make out a single word, though it tended to be high and slow, betokening men bred in bare country, and unafraid of rough weather. They had taken due precautions before they settled, for sentries were visible against the lower clouds, and all along the high road.

As the two Englishmen watched, in silence, a man on a black horse came riding through the feasters, towards the bank, and that he was a person of some consequence was proclaimed by the fact that as he passed parties, fellows who had been sitting cross-legged, crouched over the fires or resting on their elbows, all with one consent rose nimbly, and followed him. Under the tree from which the sheep-skins waved, he turned his horse, and facing towards his array, held up a hand for silence. To his surprise, Little John found that, had he been nearer, he, or any Englishman, could have understood all that this man said. For although many of the words which he used were unfamiliar, his speech was clear as a bugle call, and that of a lord that has seen courts outside his own country. He spoke very slowly, and without using ges-

ture to drive his japes home, and when he paused, his
listeners laughed heartily; another thing to surprise
Little John, who had always been told that there were no
jokes in Scotland.   But of all that the outlaw strained his
ears to catch, only two sentences were distinctly audible.
At the end of a passage in which the lord must have
praised his followers, he told them: 'We have not come
this length for nought.'   His last sentence, before he
dismissed them, was: 'And the morn's morn, a Queen
shall break her fast with ye.'

He turned his horse again, to ride away, and Little
John saw his features outlined against the sky, and saw
that his mein was high, and his countenance was marvellously dark.   Neither moonlight nor firelight woke a
gleam in his armour, which seemed to be painted black.
He twisted round in his saddle, and stared for a moment
into the forest depths, and Little John caught his breath;
for never had he seen so purposeful a light shine in such
dark eyes, under so sombre a brow.

Men began to slip from the camp, down into the surrounding country.   One of them passed so close to Robin
Hood and Little John that, catching a foot in a bramble-
strand, he nearly fell upon them.   Too soon, in Little
John's opinion, Robin rose, and began to follow this man,
saying: 'We must snare this bird.'   But this was a matter
easier said than performed, for the Scot moved like a deer,
and seemed nothing daunted that he was in strange
country and by fitful moonlight.   Little John's respect
for the invaders grew as minutes passed, and still the
light-footed Scot was to be seen, at intervals, slipping
uphill and down, halted neither by brake, dyke, fosse,
stream, nor rock.   He became aware that he was followed
(as was inevitable) when they had to draw up close behind

him in a tanglewood, but he did not lose his head.   He
tried to throw them off, very craftily, and might have
succeeded, but that ill luck led him down to the very path
by which they had ascended after meeting the shepherd,
not two hours past.   They cornered him at last at the edge
of the mere.   'I want to hear him speak,' quoth Robin to
Little John, as they separated, so, as Little John swung
down upon the figure twisting and turning over-knees
in mud, he called out in friendly guise: 'Good even, good
sir.   Have you lost your road?'

The Scot saw that he was lost indeed.   His hand
sprang from his belt to his stocking, but he could not,
for mire, draw forth the knife that he doubtless kept there.
When Robin appeared, on the other side of him, offering
him a hand to pull him to dry land, he did not scorn it.
For a second they all stood panting at one another, then
Robin asked softly: 'Who is your lord up yonder, and on
what errand has he sent you?'

The Scot pushed his red hair out of his eyes and stood
like a stag at bay, but answered nothing.   'Come, come,'
said Little John, taking him by the upper arm and shaking
him gently, 'you must answer my master,' whereupon
the Scot spake, but gave another question instead of an
answer: 'Furrst, what may be your name, surr?'   At that
Robin, startling Little John too, said right pleasantly:
'In Sherwood I am known as Robin Hood.'   'Och!'
exclaimed the Scot.   'Weel, I've hearrd on ye.   Weel,
to-night ye have seen the guid Lorrd James and ten
thousand of his men—I speak of the Black Douglas,'
he ended haughtily.

His voice was loud; the ground above was soft.
Otherwise, three men so wary would not have been taken
unprepared by a company on horseback.   The Scot's

roar had scarcely died when a precise English voice from above ordered: 'There are three of them! Seize them'; and, as afterwards will appear, this was the encounter which decided Robin Hood to enlist a Scot amongst his merry men, and a Scot to cleave to Robin Hood and leave his own land. For these three outlaws, united so strangely, served ten men-at-arms of William of Melton's company such good blows in the water meadows of Fryston that a song was made of the fight. The contest was not long, for they were outnumbered from the first, but before it was done, the Scot, seizing them in his long arms, had tossed two men out of their saddles and into the mere, and Robin Hood and Little John, fighting back to back, had laid low three more. But this still left five fresh, armed men against three, lightly armed and weary, and along the mereside came the sound of trotting hooves, which heralded a party of twenty more. The Scot gasped: 'Gude faith! they fight on every side.' The company closed around Robin, calling him 'False Scot!' and he gave himself up, only protesting: 'If you continue to call me Scot I will fight to the death.' As they disputed amongst themselves he flung an order to Little John: 'Put Jockey to sleep'; then he entreated his captors: 'Take me to your master.'

The man who sat on a tall white horse, on the knoll above the mere, was well known by sight to Robin, for he was the Archbishop of York, William of Melton. He looked passing long, dressed in warlike array (for he had taken the field against the Scots invaders), and to tell truth, when men disturbed his bones, five hundred years after he had been honourably buried, and took away from his tomb his chalice and paten, which he had caused to be enclosed with him, those bones still measured six feet.

In life he was very benevolent, ate and drank sparingly,. gathered considerable gold, and seldom changed countenance. He took one look at Robin and said: 'This man is no Scot!' He was a learned man, cunning in several tongues, and had seen several capitals, nevertheless, his English was that of the port of Hull, where he had been born of humble parents. He fixed his gaze on Robin's face, and said:'Explain yourself,' to which Robin answered gladly, with a bow: 'My Lord Archbishop, I am no Scot, but while I and my fellow, who are honest citizens of Berwick, took our revenge upon a Scot, your company,. coming upon us suddenly, tried to slay us. So we defended ourselves, as men must.' The Archbishop,. without withdrawing his gaze, commanded some of his people: 'Bring up the Scot for question.' 'Alack!' said Robin, stopping him, 'that would be vain. He will never speak again.' And when he was next able to look back over his shoulder, he saw that Little John had acted well, and as he had been told. The Scot now lay on his back in the mire, and Little John had reverently covered his visage with a neckcloth, and folded his arms on his breast, so that he was ready for carriage for burial.

'But, my lord,' continued Robin, laying a hand on the scarlet trappings of the Archbishop's horse, 'let me break to you something which you should presently know.' It was in a very loud voice that he announced: 'The Scots lord called Black Douglas, with ten thousand wild men, is a hundred miles further south than ye deem in Pomfret. He is not a league from this spot where we stand, encamped on a moor; and he has sent scouts running down to see how well the palace of Brotherton is guarded. And I myself have heard him promise his men that to-morrow a Queen shall break her fast with them.'

The Archbishop, as was his custom, scarcely showed that he had heard something which caused him great wonder. He searched Robin's face, and found it honest. Yet, since he was a man of wisdom, something troubled him. At length he asked: 'Citizen of Berwick, you say. . . . How are you called?'

'My name is Gamble Gold, my lord,' said Robin, 'and I have not seen my house these sixteen months; ever since the Scots——'

The Archbishop interrupted him: 'Well, Gamble Gold, you will come with me, you and your fellow, down to Brotherton. And there you may lie this night, while I test whether your tale be true.' He stood in his stirrups, and gave some curt orders, sending some men in this direction and some in that, to search for the Scots. He himself turned down towards Brotherton, which proved, to the outlaws' relief, a very short way from the meadows of Fryston, had they but known the road. Even so, the first of the prelate's scouts caught up the party which he led as it reached the palace doors. Robin Hood and Little John, who had been obliged to trot alongside the Archbishop's tall horse, were not sorry when a man, coming at the gallop, cried that the Berwick fellow's tale was honest as day. A Scots army was within two leagues of England's Queen.

After that the night was full of confusion, and Robin Hood and Little John, munching cold pasties and drinking good ale, in a lower chamber of the gatehouse, saw much flickering of torches outside, and many varlets running hither and thither, calling out. The outlaws thought it prudent not to take their departure with any appearance of haste, so they ate and drank their fill of the good fare sent down to them, and when he was full Little John put something for breakfast in his pocket. They left softly, with the dawn, nobody hindering them, and as they did so, they heard the splash of oars, and perceived that a barge was pushing off from the water-gate of the palace, and amongst the persons crouched in it were certainly ladies, but so hooded and muffled that nobody could see their faces.

So it befell that the Black Douglas did not capture the Queen of England, as he had sworn. According to a chronicler called John de Trokelowe, she made her escape by water, to Nottingham—a thing impossible, unless she took to the road for passage between several rivers. This Trokelowe wrote his history twelve years after the event, and was a monk of St. Albans, but if it is correct that he was formerly of the priory of Tynemouth, in Northumberland, as some think, he may have heard true tales from the north country. Another chronicler, a monk of the Abbey of Malmesbury, wrote that she was removed first to York, for safety; but to get to York, she must have travelled very perilously, through country overrun by invading Scots. The sad part of this history is that the expedition which had sought to carry her captive, when it was brought to battle by the warlike Archbishop at a place called Myton, on the River Swayle, on the twelfth day of that September, utterly defeated William of Melton. The King was forced to leave off besieging Berwick, and it was whispered that his cousin of Lancashire had been bribed by the Scots.

The merry part of this history concerns Robin Hood and his Scotsman. Poor Jock was still in the moist place where they had left him when the outlaws returned there, in great haste, with growing daylight. The sun was coming through, and the birds were singing, and the day

See page 180

Maid Marian . . . would disappear with the outlaws into the
greenwood, to learn forest secrets and woodcraft

was going to be very fine. The Scot was sitting up, and feeling himself all over. Sunlight displayed that his matted hair was the colour of flames. He had high cheekbones, large brown eyes, like many beasts but not so many men, and a jaw like a pudding, because of the blow that Little John had dealt him, to put him to sleep. Yet it seemed that he bore no malice, for his first words to Robin were: 'Gude master, I am henceforth your man!' He rose to his feet, and was seen as a stout fellow, nigh as tall as Little John. He said solemnly: 'My name is Alexander!'

Robin Hood laughed, and said: 'You are well named, for you are as good a fighter as any man I ever met. But if I were to take you into my company, you would surely be false to me.'

'I am verra grateful to your lang loon for dealing me this buffet,' proceeded the Scot doggedly, 'for I fancy the priest in armour would have used torture to make me speak. And I would never have spoken.'

'Why, so I fancied,' agreed Robin Hood. 'But what of your faith to your lord, the Black Douglas?'

'Speak to me no more of any Douglas,' said the Scot, looking terrible. In a mutter he explained: 'Two Douglases slew two of my cousins on our road here. They fell out over a sheep.'

'Then thou hast not been true to sire or cuz,' said Robin.

'Not so,' said the Scot. 'For, as my duty to my cuz, I slew four Douglases; and although the gude Lord James is a bonny fighter, so are you. Moreover, he has promised, if I survive the battle that is to be, he will hang me.'

When Robin Hood heard this, and saw the man look

so rueful, he stretched his limbs, for he was weary, and said: 'Well, I have heard it is ill talking between a full man and a fasting. Little John, give Alexander somewhat out of your pouch.'

And after a few weeks' trial, finding the Scot fleet, faithful, and a man of his hands (though somewhat slow in the uptake), he admitted him to his band.

The Scot asked to be addressed as Alexander on Feast Days, which was done accordingly, but answered to 'Sandy' on lesser occasions. Unfortunately, he pronounced this 'Sawndey,' and so it came that the band, and generations of Englishmen thereafter, came to call every Scot, come south, 'a Sawney,' and (until they found out their mistake) believed them to be as simple as they looked.

PART FOUR

ROBIN, MARIAN & THE KING

THE autumn rains came down out of skies dark as the
ocean on a stormy day, and all leaves fell from the trees
in Barnesdale.   In the forest rival harts were meeting.
They fought in the moonlight with clashing antlers and
dilated eyes, their fierce hooves furrowing the soft wet
earth.   The news in England that season was dark too,
for the King had recalled his favourite, one Hugo
Despenser, who had been a pirate on the high seas ever
since the King's counsellors, headed by the crafty Bishop
of Hereford, had compelled their master to banish him.
The King was marching north, at the head of an army,
said to be thirty thousand strong, and the lords of the
north, led by his cousin the Earl of Lancaster, were
besieging the royal castle of Tickhill that stood in the
country between Sherwood and Barnesdale.

Robin Hood, taking only Little John with him, wintered
by the seaside in the North Riding of Yorkshire.   It may
have been that, like many in England, although he loved
the name of the King, he did not love the name of the
King's favourite, and thought the King's cousin had
some right upon his side.

Robin and Little John spent a Holy Yule-tide with good
Abbot Richard in the Abbey of St. Hilda at Whitby.
After dinner on Christmas Day, which was a day of spark-
ling white frost and sunshine, they entertained the com-
munity with a display of archery.   Each outlaw drew his
bowstring to his ear, and shot a flight arrow from the
square tower of the abbey church.   They descended
from the tower, accompanied by the Abbot and monks in

procession.   After some search they found both arrows on
the far side of a lane at Hawsker, a place the monks were
sure was more than a measured mile from their abbey.
Abbot Richard decreed that a pillar should be set up to
mark the spot where each arrow had fallen, and that the
meadows in which they lay should henceforward be known
as 'Robinsfield' and 'Johnspiece.'

With the New Year Robin parted from Little John, and
passed south to an obscure fishing village with a sandy
bay.   Here he sought amongst the fishermen's dwellings
for a lodging, giving his name as Simon from over the
Lee.   He said further that he was a poor fisherman from
the south, a single man, and prepared to be handy about
the house.   A widow woman, who had a cottage overlooking the great grey waters of the North Sea, took him
in gladly.   She owned a good boat, a little herring buss,
but was dissatisfied with the master whom she had hired
to sail it since her husband's death.   She suspected the
man of having an arrangement with his crew to part
profits ere anything came her way.   She told Robin to go
out with them, and offered him a small wage for doing so.
Robin served her also in many other ways for which he
was not paid.   On evenings unmeet for fishing, when
there were wild white horses at sea, he would sit in her
house, outlined against a window-full of sky, green and
blue as dusk meadows in May-time.   By the yellow light
of a tallow dip he mended her long, tangled fishing-nets
which were rust-red as the head he bent over them.   The
widow looked at his intent side-face and thought him a
proper fellow.   She said:

'Simon, wouldst thou not like to have a boat of thine
own?'

Robin tightened a knot with his white teeth, looking

dangerous, but answered, mild as milk, that he had never thought on such a thing.

'Think of it now,' said the dame.   'For your name is a good one for a fisherman.'

'My name!' exclaimed Robin.

'Simon!   Simon!' said she, wagging her knitting at him.   'I believe you were not so christened.'

'I know,' said he, 'that you were not there to hear.'

At that she bridled, for truly she had the more years in her dish.

'I am also persuaded,' she said, 'that you are not a single man.'

'There,' answered Robin calmly, 'you are certainly wrong.'

'Then,' said she, 'you should think shame of yourself, for the world is bursting full of fair maidens lacking men. And I believe you would not make so ill a husband.'

'Little you know,' said Robin Hood.

The widow advanced and showed him what she had been knitting, which was a fisherman's cap, with a long tail ending in a tassel, red as fire and as warm.

'"Tis for you, Simon,' said she.   'I could not bear to see you going forth in my boat in such foul weather with no cap, poor lad.'

'*Gramerci*, dame!' said Robin, fitting it on.   'Now I have such a cap, I must think of courting some maids.'

Next day the storm had abated, and he sailed away in the widow's boat, which was called the *Blithe*, taking provisions for several days.   But while the rest of the crew cast baited hooks over her side, Robin sat letting down bare lines into the deep seas.   The crew winked at one another, 'Simon's in love,' and the master hired by the widow was furious, because he had thought of wooing her himself, for love of her boat. He said to Robin:

'What are you about? It will be long, you great lubber, ere you thrive at sea. I promise you that you shall have no part of our fish on this journey.'

'I grieve,' said Robin dreamily, 'the day I came to these parts. Would that I were in Plumpton Park, chasing the fallow deer.'

'Hark to my lord, the noble fisherman!' jeered the master. 'Well, you will soon long more than ever that you were on dry land, for we are running into another storm.'

This they did, and at the end of three days' tossing, found themselves out of known waters, and under a dawn sky the colour of primroses. The only other thing in the world to be seen, except air and water, was a ship of war, bearing down upon them. She had two great masts with square sails painted with strange devices, and a stage at her stern, for fighting men, and another forward, and a great rudder moved by means of a tiller.

The master of the *Blithe* spat into the sea, and cursed the day that he had been born. 'We may count every fish we have on board lost to us,' said he, 'for yonder ship is a French pirate. And what is worse, we shall, like as not, all spend the rest of our lives in a vile-smelling French prison.'

Robin Hood dropped the hand with which he had been shading his eyes while he looked at the handsome ship, and said softly: 'Give me my bent bow in my hand, and never a Frenchman will I spare.'

The master burst out angrily: 'Will you hold your peace, you bragging long lubber? I am well minded to lighten our craft by casting you overboard.'

At that Robin arose and drew his long bow.   A silver-nocked arrow sped upwards, and in the castle on the top-mast of the French ship a little man spread out his hands and fell to his knees.   Robin fitted another arrow, and another, and two more men on board the pirate bowed as it were to him, and dropped on to their faces.   A third man, who received an arrow in the shoulder, toppled sideways and fell into the sea.

Robin ticked his tongue in his teeth, and called to the master of the little *Blithe*:

'Master!   Seek not to flee our enemy, for she is but slightly manned and by fellows of small cunning.   But tie me to the mast that I may shoot fair.   I am a poor lubber, not accustomed to leaping timbers under my soles as I take aim.'

The master ordered his crew to bind Robin fast to the mast, and while the *Blithe* bobbed amongst the crystal waters of the great North Sea that dawn, Robin Hood, taking steady aim, sent arrows into the hearts of a dozen Frenchmen.   At last he picked off the captain of the pirate ship, as he stood on the stern-stage, where-upon her crew, crying out that the green archer was a devil, took to the ship's boats.   Too many frightened fellows tried to embark, and all sank forthwith.   After that had befallen, Robin led the crew of the *Blithe* aboard their prize.

They brought her back into Scarborough harbour the next Sunday afternoon, and many people in their best clothes ran down to see the French pirate captured by Simon from over the Lee.   The master of the *Blithe* said:

'She should be yours, Simon, and indeed you should be known as the Noble Fisherman.   But what will you do with a ship of war?'

'One half of her,' said Robin merrily, 'I shall keep for my wife and small children.   The other I mean to bestow upon all that were my fellows at sea.'

He was as good as his word, for he parted half of the money he got for his prize amongst the master and crew of the *Blithe*.   But his own half he spent ordering a seemly chapel of white stone to be dedicated to St. Mary Magdalen.   Afterwards he went to the widow's house to gather his gear.   He said that he was going to live inland awhile.

He left the widow's house on a bright March morning. The wind was so sharp that it brought tears into the dame's eyes as she gave him her hand in farewell.   She said:

'Welladay, Simon, now will you go courting a maid?'

He answered her gravely at last: 'Ah! dame, I did my courting seasons past, but it was not God's will that the business should end in joy-bells.   Pray for all sworn bachelors!'

Then he took the road over the wolds towards the west.

THE outlaws assembled that spring in a part of Sherwood called Birkland, where the soil was red as last
season's bracken, and there were glades amid slender
silver birch-trees, and great oaks so ancient that they had
seen the priests of Old England—men armed with sickle-
shaped knives, dressed in long white garments, with hair
white as wool crowned with ivy leaves, and long beards
dyed bright blue.

Robin rejoined his band on a day of spring sunshine,
when the yellow gorse was in bloom.   His trysting place
was a major oak, thirty feet round, with branches which
spread two hundred and seventy yards.   Under its
lemon-pale budding branches he sat, and heard how his
men had wintered, and the news of the countryside.

The tidings from Barnesdale were all of confusion,
death, and disaster.   There had been a battle at Borough-
bridge, a fortnight before, after which the King's great
enemy, his rebellious cousin, had been taken prisoner.
He had been hurried to his own proud castle of Pomfret,
where the King himself had presided over a trial, said to
have been both hasty and irregular.   Thomas of Lancaster had been refused a hearing, and condemned to
die as a traitor.   Next morning, mounted on a sorry nag,
he had been led to a slight hill outside Pomfret town, and
there beheaded.

Most of Robin Hood's men had known him by sight,
for he had been the greatest lord of the country round
Barnesdale, a square-headed, heavy-fisted, somewhat
brutal-looking man of forty odd.   It had shaken the
north to think that royal blood should meet so dire an

end, and many of the earl's followers, now hiding from the King's vengeance on the moors, said that although he had been a harsh master, yet he had died in defence of the liberties of England. Now the King's favourites should misrule again. The King, after ordering thirty more executions—of lesser folk—and arresting the Bishop of Hereford, had moved up to York, whence he had summoned a Parliament.

Robin Hood took into his band under the major oak on the morning of his return three strangers, all proved men with the quarter-staff, broadsword, and long bow. When they had shown their skill, which was excellent, he asked their names. They answered that they were Will Stoutly, Jacques Hardstaff, and Bill Beardall.

Robin said, with his hawk-look: 'Whether these names be real or adopted, I ask not. Neither will I know why three such skilled fellows are masterless men. I mell me not in the quarrels of kings and their kin, whereby Merry England is torn in twain. But will ye swear on the Rood to worship God Almighty, the Saints, and particularly Our Blessed Lady, to aid the weak and needy with all your strength, to hold in reverence all women and weak persons, and to obey your captain without question?'

They all said that such was their desire, and were straightway admitted outlaws.

Then Alan a Dale came forwards, leading his wife, who had a bundle in her arms. He said: 'Captain, will you enrol one more stranger in your meinie?'

'What is his skill and his name?' said Robin.

'Marry,' said Alan a Dale, 'he has neither as yet.' Fair Annet displayed that what she bore in her arms was a male child in swaddling bands. He was three months old, she said, but they had waited to christen him 'Robin' until Friar Tuck could perform the ceremony and the captain stand his sponsor. So they had a christening in Birkland on the day of Robin Hood's home-coming.

At the feast afterwards, Much the miller's son said to his master: 'Captain, if you would enrol yet another stout fellow in your band, you should vanquish the Pindar of Wakefield at quarter-staff play.'

'And who,' said Robin, 'is the Pindar of Wakefield?'

'He is called,' answered Much, 'George a Green, because it is his duty to impound in the pin-fold in front of his dwelling, all cattle found wandering. He boasts that neither knight, squire, nor baron dares let a beast trespass on the manor of which he is guardian, because he has the stoutest arm in Yorkshire. He is betrothed to one Beatrice, the daughter of Justice Grimes, and in her honour challenges all comers with the quarter-staff. She is indeed a well enough coloured maid, and had I been a marrying man myself, I should have regretted the drubbing I got.'

'Did this Pindar indeed give our Much a drubbing?' said Robin, with a light in his eye.

Little John grunted in Much's ear: 'What devil prompted you to tell Robin of a champion at Wakefield? You know the country thereabout is quick with soldiery hunting for fugitives.' Aloud he said: 'Captain, I can ply a staff. May I go seek George a Green?'

'You may not,' said Robin, 'because your inches would betray us. I shall go alone. But rest assured, no man shall know me.'

Next morning a knight in armour of the newest fashion rode early out of Birkland. He wore a shining breast-plate over his coat of chain mail, roundels of steel on his shoulders, arm-pieces and leg-pieces of steel, and, on his head, a pointed basinet. His surcoat bore the device of a green tree torn up by the roots, and his steed was a fine bay charger.

'Were it not for the horse,' said Much to himself, as he struggled to his feet, 'I should doubt my eyes.' He rubbed the sleep out of his eyes, and added: 'I am surely man to the maddest master in Christendom. Who but Robin would adventure himself as a stranger knight, into country where every stranger is suspect?'

Much, whose conscience was pricking him, hastily saddled his own dapple-grey cob, and spurred through the forest glades after his captain. He came in sight of him again more than an hour later, just about to ford the River Ryton. On the opposite side of the ford waited another knight in armour, sitting still as a statue. Robin shouted at the boding figure, and getting no reply, rode through the ford with lance couched. The silent stranger lowered his weapon waveringly and too late to prevent himself being borne from his saddle. But as his weapon shivered, it grazed Robin's cheek.

Much splashed through the ford after his master, in time to hear Robin cry, as he straddled above his fallen adversary: 'Rise freely, young sir!' But the slight figure on the ground answered with a high shriek: 'Robin!'

The knight, who was a lady in disguise, sat on the banks of Ryton staring at Robin Hood, who had dropped on his knees. She said, drawing heavy mail gauntlets off long carven fingers: 'Well, you are a gentle lover!'

'What in the name of the saints, madam, are you doing in this guise and country?' asked Robin harshly.

'I was seeking for you,' said the lady coolly, beginning

to unbuckle her helmet. 'For my uncle, whom you know well enough, has been upon the losing side this season, and has been summoned to York to answer to the King for his misdeeds. And I know well enough that his answer will be his heiress-ward as bride for one of the King's ill companions. So last night I chucked up a penny, to see whether I should go take the veil at a nunnery in the south, or adventure myself in search of the only man in this world in whom I can put trust. The coin fell for the outlaw.'

'You deserved to be slain,' said Robin.

'The saints have decreed that I shall suffer no more than a prick in the side,' said the lady, scrambling to her feet. 'Nay, 'tis naught, nor the first you have given me. And I see that I have drawn blood from your cheek. That, I own, is unusual before the wedding.'

She shook her long hair out of her helmet, and it fell to her knees like a mantle. It was straight as rain and red as copper in firelight. Much, watching unnoticed with the horses, by a bush of the riverside, knew in his heart that here, in spirit as well as in colour, was a mate fit for his master.

'Will you wed me now, sweet Robin?' asked the lady, looking up at the prince of outlaws with a smile.

'Nay, madam,' said Robin, looking away from her.

'I am almost tired of getting that answer,' said she. 'After three years I had hoped for a change in your tune. Have you no chaplain in your band?'

'I have, and a good one,' admitted Robin.

'Well, I dare say I shall find him more reasonable,' said she. 'Now let us mount and go home.'

'You cannot live with outlaws in Sherwood, madam,' said Robin, not moving an inch.

'Why not,' said she. 'I think I was born an outlaw myself. Besides, where else can I go at present?'

She walked off towards the horses, and discovering Much, said to him: 'Are you my lord's squire? How are you called?'

'My name is Much, most haut dame,' said Much, louting low to her.

'I have come to dwell in Sherwood amongst your master's band, Much,' said the lady. 'You may call me Maid Marian.'

There never was such a merry summer as that which followed. The outlaws, looking back upon it, always spoke of the first season Maid Marian spent amongst them as the Golden Year.

Whilst a forest lodge, of which she was to be sole mistress, was being built for her, Maid Marian abode with Alan a Dale and his wife. Despite her infant, Annet gladly offered to be handmaid to the stranger lady who had come amongst them dressed in shining armour. But the day after Maid Marian had been led with music to her new-built garlanded lodge, Robin Hood rode away, leaving no word as to his home-coming.

He reappeared a week later, bringing with him George a Green, who had a black eye, and fair Beatrice Grimes, now the Pindar's bride. Fair Beatrice, after she had been presented to Maid Marian and looked long at her, said softly to Robin Hood: 'No wonder you won!'

She herself was, as Much had reported, a well enough coloured girl, with nut-brown hair, short and curly, like that of a page, and a rosebud mouth and rolling blue eyes. She was little and merry, like a robin. Beside Maid Marian she appeared as a star attendant on the moon, a daisy sprung near a lily, or a pool of rain water compared to the deep and changeful sea. Indeed there could be no comparison between them. She also gladly became Maid Marian's tirewoman, and it was soon evident that this lady would provide enough work for a couple of damsels in waiting, besides a score or so of willing serving-men.

Annet and Beatrice listened pop-eyed, while their mistress told them with high-born candour that she was eighteen, and though she had been betrothed four times, still a maid.

'I seem to be fatal to suitors,' said she. 'As soon as my guardian has marketed me to his pleasure, the bridegroom takes ill and dies, generally of old age. I am sorry for the gentlemen, but one cannot greatly grieve for people one has never seen, and the only one of them on whom I ever set eyes wanted me to give up hunting because it is unsafe.'

She could sew little coloured silk flowers, so like nature that you almost bent to pick them off their background, and cherubim with blown-back hair of gold-thread, and lions and leopards with lolling tongues and jewelled eyes. But she had no idea how to darn a ladder in knit hose, or put a patch under the arm of a worn gown. She had brought with her into the greenwood a necklace of pearls, each as large as a marble, which she continually left hanging over the foot of her bed. As for her balas ruby, the size of a pigeon's egg, which she sometimes wore hanging round her neck from a chain of emeralds, she pressed it upon Alan a Dale as a present for his wife, so that their infant could cut his teeth on it. She let the child do this often, while she dandled him on her knee, singing to him songs Alan would have been glad to learn.

She had never seen an egg boiled or a hen plucked, and seemed to expect banquets to descend from the skies at any hour, lowered by heavenly hands. But she wasted little daylight sewing, singing, or eating, for every moment she could she spent out of doors, fencing, drawing the long bow, and even essaying to play at single-staff. She rode cross-saddle, like a young lord, knew every point of horse, hawk, and hound, and was beloved by all. Once, when a mettlesome steed bucked her off in midstream of a river, she swam to shore, cool as a mermaid. Her favourite dress was a page's doublet and hose. Thus attired she would disappear with the outlaws into the greenwood, to learn forest secrets and woodcraft. They showed her the new-born red-deer calves, lying quiet and bright-eyed in deep bracken, and the pretty creatures, knowing as yet no fear of man, would suck her fingers. She learnt to know the track of the hind from that of the hart, and to tell, from the width and depth of a slot, the age and weight of the beast that had left it. Wise men whispered to her the Hart-Royal's lair, harbour, and soiling-pool, and led her to see the fallow deer's sunning-bed. She saw the young staggarts shedding their horns as they browsed in the April glades, and looking as much shocked as a lady whose hat has blown off. Later in the season she watched the same gentlemen at work on branch and rail, rubbing worn grey velvet from their fine new antlers.

She saw the old hind gravely leading through the coppices five or six daughters, all with a great look of *Madame Mère*, and the hunted hart running down-wind in the midst of a parcel of fleeing dames, his noble head held low to hide his towering points. She knew already how to take fish from streams with her angle, and which trees

*Every moment she could she spent out of doors, fencing, drawing
the long bow . . .*

and shrubs were likely food, screen, and covert for beasts
of the chase and venery, and which for rascals.   She
astonished her companions by the speed and ease with
which she picked up their weather-lore.

'*Gramerci!*' Maid Marian would smile, as she stepped
out of her lodge very early, dressed for a day of sport.
'Gossamer on the sward, cobwebs from brake to brake,
and a low dawn.   We shall have fine weather this day.'
Or again, as she trailed her green skirts indoors from the
supper table: 'Cocks crowing at Papplewick, cattle and
sheep tail to wind, and a rippled sky!   To-morrow, Alan,
I will teach your minstrels the French hunting song.'

But there were so few wet days that summer, a man
might have counted them on the fingers of one hand.
Maid Marian was able to plan the contests and expeditions
in which her soul delighted, weeks ahead.   May Day, she
said, was her birthday.   'I know it is not held a lucky
month for maids, gentlemen, but I have ever held it
better to be bold than lucky.   Therefore let us keep my
birthday bravely.'

She ordered a tilting display in a crescent-shaped
meadow at the forest edge for the morning of that day,
after High Mass.   For the afternoon her scheme was
an archery contest, and wrestling, followed by a banquet
and evensong.   The hours of fading daylight, she said,
might be given up to juggling, harping, and dancing.
It seemed, indeed, as she complained to Annet and
Beatrice, that she had not been formed by nature to end
her days in a cloister. 'And yet,' said she with a sigh, as
they laced her gown of green silk and braided her pearls
in her long plaits of red gold, 'that is just what I seem
like to do!'

WHILE Fair Annet and Beatrice a Green were attiring
Maid Marian in a green silk robe, in a forest lodge, two
damsels in a castle of Barnesdale were putting off their
silk gowns and getting into doublet and hose of hodden
grey cloth.

They were sisters, and the elder, who was much the
taller, had springing bright gold curls and a rosy mouth
and roses in her cheeks. Her lady mother, who had
loved her dearly, had caused her to be christened Rose,
and always dressed her in gowns of rose-red. The
younger, who was much under the middle height, and so
slightly made that she looked more like a child of ten
than a damsel of sixteen, had locks of palest gold, straight
as rain, and no colour in her cheeks, so her mother had
caused her to be christened Lily, and always dressed her
in gowns of no colour.

But alas! the mother who had loved so well these
flowers of hers, died untimely, and their father rode south
to the King's court, at Westminster, and brought back
to them as stepdame a widow of London city, who had
the voice of a peacock, and small eyes like black beads,
and was so portly that she made floors tremble. This
widow had been richly left by an old merchant, and not
the least of her treasures were her two comely sons.
When first she came to their castle in Barnesdale the
damsels did not mislike her, for she used them kindly
while their father was nigh, and she had brought them
two jolly playmates. But as the years passed the
damsels came to like their stepdame less and less, and
her sons more and more, and at length, on an April day,

Bold Arthur came to his mother and told her that he loved Rose the Red, and Brave Willy said that he had plighted his troth with White Lily.

The damsels' stepdame was a very secret woman. When she heard these tidings she did not say anything. She made as if her sons had told her no more than that the year was at the spring.   But she went into her solar chamber, and Patch, the castle fool, who had dearly loved his first mistress, the damsels' mother, heard her walking up and down and speaking, although she was alone.   And he trembled.

Next day she came to her elder son and told him that she had heard from her lord, in London, and that he said that the Court was likely to come to Nottingham next season.   She said that though it would grieve her sore to part with her Bold Arthur, she thought that as he was full grown it would be good for him, and pleasant, that he should see a little of the world beyond Barnesdale. He was startled at this, but so relieved that she said nothing against his speech of yesterday, that he quickly said he would do her bidding, and go to London.   He said to her in farewell: 'It grieves me as sorely to go as it does you to part with me.'   He kissed her hand and bade her: 'Never be worse to Rose the Red than you have been to me.'

So Bold Arthur rode away to see more of the world after a very sorrowful parting with Rose the Red, and next day the stepdame called her younger son to her, and said: 'Now that your brother is departed, the days will seem long to you.   From a child you have always said that you would like to sail the sea.   It will nigh break my heart to part with you, but your uncle, the merchant of London Town, has written that he is going in a ship of

his, this month, to Tripoli.   And for the love of me, he
says he will take a son of mine, who shall be as his own
son; for he has no heir.'

It was true that from a child Brave Willy had desired
to sail the sea, and he knew that he was but a younger son
of small inheritance.   So after a very sorrowful parting
with White Lily, he kissed his mother's hand, and said
in farewell: 'Never be worse to White Lily than you
were to me.'

No sooner were both her sons gone than the stepdame
began to ill-use her stepdaughters.   She had spoken
truth when she said that it grieved her sore to part with
her sons.   Her aim now was to break the hearts of Rose
the Red and White Lily.   She smiled as she asked them
why they had ceased to sing so loud all day as they had
been wont to do.   She smiled when they took up silent
mourning and would not answer her mockery.   At
nights she stood listening outside their chamber door, to
hear what they said to one another when they thought
no one in the castle was awake.   But she learned nothing
by this means, for Patch, the fool, who could slip about
the castle like a kit, a withered autumn leaf, or a shadow,
had warned them never to break their minds to one
another, or speak of their loves, except when he was by
to keep guard.

At the end of a year a messenger came to the castle,
bearing a letter from the damsel's father, to say that
the Court was coming to Nottingham.   The messenger
brought out of his bosom another letter, which he said
that his young master had told him to give into the hand
of Rose the Red.   The stepdame smiled and said that
she would save him the trouble.   The fool, who was
in the hall, though she knew it not, saw her tear open that

letter, and smile again as she dropped it into the fire. She then went up alone into her solar chamber, and the fool heard her walking up and down and talking to herself. He hurried to the damsels, and told them what he had heard and seen; and White Lily, although she was the smaller and the younger, bade him get for them secretly, many ells of coarse hodden grey cloth, and shoes that were stout.   She said to her sister: 'Why should we stay in Barnesdale to waste our youth in pain? You and I will to the greenwood to live with Robin Hood and his merry men.   All say that he will not suffer wrong to be done to those that are weak and forlorn, and love Our Lady.'

'By my faith,' said Rose the Red, 'you speak well.   We will take the fool, for escort, and dress ourselves plainly, like village maidens, in gowns and cloaks of hodden grey.'

'Not so,' said White Lily.   'You and I must now as young gallants go.   We will put on doublet and hose, and cut our yellow hair as page-boys do.   And I will wear a sword on my hip, and a dagger in my belt; and the fool shall teach us to swear.'

The fool agreed to do this, and he got them many ells of coarse grey stuff, which they sewed by candle-light with much pain, in their own bower, while he kept guard. But they began to sing all day again, and this made their stepdame curious.   She therefore told them that Bold Arthur, when next they saw him, would be a wedded man. He was happily promised to a merchant's daughter of London Town, and the pair were going to be married, with much feasting, at St. Mary's Church, when the Court came to Nottingham.   She said that she would be taking them both to see, and that they should strew rose-petals in the bride's path—for this was the nearest to a

husband or a wedding that either of them was ever like
to come.   They disbelieved all she said, but they ceased
to sing.

On a May night, when the horned moon was tracing
silver on every whispering tree top, about the tenth hour
of the night, when every soul in the castle was asleep,
the damsels arrayed themselves in doublet and hose
and folded away their robes of silk.   They stained each
other's faces with an umber dye, which the fool had got
for them: Rose the Red wore a curtal-axe upon her thigh,
and took a boar spear in her hand; White Lily slung
behind her a minstrel's harp, and they gave to Patch a
small bundle tied up in a handkerchief, to be fastened
to a stick.   This contained all their jewels and gold.   As
they stole out of doors White Lily laughed and, 'I
wonder,' said she, 'what our stepdame would say, gin
she this sight could see!'

But two days later, when they found themselves safe
in Sherwood forest, they were not too merry.   'Oh!
Jupiter!' quoth Rose the Red, 'how weary are my spirits!'

'I care not for my spirits,' said Patch, 'if my legs were
not so weary.'

'I pray you, bear with me,' said White Lily, 'I can go
no further.'   They seated themselves beneath a tree,
and the damsels began to compare their blisters.

'I confess,' said Rose the Red, as she put on her shoon
again, 'I could find it in my heart to disgrace my man's
apparel and cry like a woman.'

'Well,' said White Lily, looking around them, 'this
is the forest of Sherwood.'

'Ay,' agreed Patch.   'Now am I in Sherwood.   The
more fool I.   When I was at home I was in a better
place.'

As they sat thus dismally, they perceived a short stout
man, in a green dress, passing adown a nearby glade,
and White Lily said: 'If either of you twain can rise to

They seated themselves beneath a tree . . .

your feet, pray question this fellow, if he for gold will
get us food.'   Neither of the others felt like rising, but
the fool called out: 'Holloa! good clown.'   'Peace, fool,
he is not thy kinsman,' said Rose the Red, and struggled
to her feet.   Much the miller's son (for it was he)
halted, and asked: 'Who calls?'   'Your betters,' answered

Patch. 'Else are they very wretched,' said Much, pinning on a sorry look as he surveyed the two jaunty golden-haired boys in hodden grey, and their odd companion. Rose the Red said very mannerly: 'Good even, friend. We would get some food and rest ourselves awhile. Can gold buy such refreshment in this desert place?'

'Fair sir,' said Much, 'I pity you. But I am not my own master. I am shepherd to another man, and do not shear the fleeces which I graze. My master,' he added, 'is of a churlish disposition, and little reckons to find his way to heaven by doing deeds of hospitality. But if you like, and if you have gold, I can lead you to him.'

White Lily asked if the way was long, and he said no, so the three footsore travellers set forth again, Much leading, and he led them to a clearing where lay five-and-twenty fine fellows dressed in Lincoln green. They were flung on the turf around a fire on which dinner was a-cooking, and one of their number, as the scent of a savoury stew stole upon the air, was singing a song in praise of the outdoor life. Much presented the travellers to the company, and said that these fair gentlemen were willing to give his master gold for their entertainment, and all the men laughed, and some winked. Patch the fool decided to sit upon the bundle which he carried, a thing he found right uncomfortable while he feasted. While they fed they heard a peal of joy-bells ring out, in the valley below, and Rose the Red sprang to her feet, and cried out distressfully: 'Oh! do those ring for a wedding at St. Mary's Kirk?' They told her, not likely. Such bells were rung when the King and his Court arrived in Nottingham town. But she could not rest again, but stood with a finger at her lip and brows perplexed.

When Patch the fool saw approaching them a man with
red hair, dressed in Lincoln green, with a hound by his
side so tall that his hand could rest on its collar, and
behind him a man so tall that he seemed a giant, he
trembled and looked aside.   But Rose the Red stood up
stoutly, and in the guise of a saucy lad greeted Robin
Hood fair.   She told him that she and her companions
were shepherds' boys out of Barnesdale, and that she was
on her road to the King's Court, her true love to see, but
that her brother and their clown were so spent that she
must ask for them some more hospitality.   Robin said:
'Shepherd boy, your accent is something finer than you
could purchase in so removed a place as Barnesdale.'
'I have been told so of many,' agreed Rose the Red.   'But
indeed an old religious uncle of mine taught me to speak,
who was in his youth an inland man.'   Much was behind
his master, mentioning: 'The gentle youths say that they
will give you gold for their entertainment, good master,'
whereat Robin's eyes twinkled, and came to rest upon
poor Patch.   But after a little more questioning, he
promised very pleasantly to find the clown and White
Lily shelter for a day or two.   Indeed, he said that they
had best stay till the month was out.   They should then
try some merry contests with his fellows, with the single
staff and cudgels, swords and bucklers.   They must
wrestle with Clym, shoot against Alan, and dive and
swim in the river with the whole company.   As he let
drop these suggestions, one by one, the damsels looked
at one another, round-eyed, and hastily away again; the
umber dye on their cheeks and brows could not disguise
their pallor, and their knees shook.   But Rose the Red,
plucking up heart, offered that her young brother should
sing a song or two, and said that she herself was fond of

all beasts.   Robin asked how she was called, and she said: 'I am Roger Round, and my brother is Nick,' whereupon he said that Will Scarlet should show Roger the way down to the town, and stay with him there till he found his true love.   He led them to the forest lodge, in front of which sat Maid Marian, with Fair Annet and Beatrice a Green, and the damsels in lad's attire brightened much in countenance when they saw so unlooked for a sight in the heart of the greenwood.

Next morning, before they parted, they took counsel together, and Will Scarlet said that every day, towards dusk, Nick Round and the clown should come to the fringe of the forest and blow a blast on a bugle.   If they heard an answering blast from the city below, they would know that he and Roger Round needed succour.

Three evenings running, White Lily and Patch went down to the forest's edge, and they grew to blow a bugle meetly.   They watched the lights begin to spring up in the far-away city, and some faint sounds of revelry floated up to them, but never an answering bugle-call. Wending their way back to the forest lodge they never met any one face to face, but sometimes they heard a twig crackle, or a branch sigh; and once, chancing to look up, White Lily noted that many a tree along the forest edge held a silent watcher lying full length amongst its greenery looking down towards the city; and the clown, once chancing to stop and bend down and tie his shoe, found that in front of what he had taken in the faint light for a solid oak, stood a green man, silent as a statue.

By the end of the third day, Patch the fool was most uneasy, for wriggle as he might, he was told that his name was set down for a wrestling match with Little John, and as for White Lily, she could no longer refuse

a bout with sword and buckler with Robin himself.
Great was their happiness when, almost before the first
blast of their bugle had died away in echo, on that third
evening, they heard an answer from close by, and up the
hill towards them came a merry company, richly dressed,
hand-linked and laughing. There was the father of the
damsels, in a long gown, with his hand in that of Rose
the Red, who with her other hand held that of Bold
Arthur, and he had Brave Willy by the arm. There
never was such a jolly meeting on the edge of the forest,
nor so much kissing and hugging, and the green men,
who had been waiting ready to lend their aid, slipped
away, like snow in a thaw, knowing that there was nothing
that they could do to aid a party so happy already. For
all in the same breath, Brave Willy was telling White
Lily how he was richly come from Tripoli, and Rose the
Red was telling her that Bold Arthur had sent letters
every month, telling his great love, but none had reached
her; and their father was saying that the King himself
had called for his horse, when he had set eyes on Rose the
Red, vowing that he must into his Sire-wood, to see if it
be truth that another page so pretty was hidden there.
However, he had been persuaded from this, on the
promise that White Lily should be fetched forth and
brought to his Court. He had sent for robes of silver
cloth and girdles of shining gold, and both the damsels
were to be wedded to their true loves at St. Mary's Kirk
next day.

Patch the fool, when he heard this last news, said:
'Now shall floors tremble in a castle in Barnesdale! I
think I should be wise to stay in Sherwood forest, and
become a green man. Only that means that I must
wrestle with Little John.'

The damsels comforted him, but carelessly, because their hearts were light, and they all departed together down to Nottingham town, singing and hand-linked.

Robin Hood watched them go, without himself being seen of them, and when he had heard from Will Scarlet of his adventures in the Court, with Rose the Red, he laughed too. It was not until he sat to sup that night, and Maid Marian, looking down the board, asked: 'Where are the Round boys and their clown?' that Robin smote his brow reproachfully, and said: 'Oh! I should have told you. They are all gone to be wedded, in Nottingham town (save the clown), and be not amazed, but those two puny boys were well-born damsels in disguise.' To this Maid Marian answered, smiling at him tenderly: 'Bless your heart!'

Patch trembled much when the bridegrooms with their brides arrived at a castle in Barnesdale, but his fears were soon blown away. For when the stepdame saw that all her arts had failed to win her sons from their true loves, and that her lord bent a heavy look on her, and that her two sons seemed not to love her as well as they had done, she was dismayed. She sought her solar chamber, and walked up and down so that the floors shook, Patch the fool observing softly. He stole up behind her, as she muttered, and plucked her sleeve and asked: 'Madam, will you run away to join Robin Hood? I can show you the way.' She called him false knave, and bade him begone on pain of a whipping; but she did not run to the greenwood. She stayed in the castle of Barnesdale, waxing larger, and kinder. She continued to walk up and down, within its walls, but no longer alone. Behind her pattered many fair children; in the fullness of time she called herself grandam of fourteen. The twelve sons of Bold Arthur and Brave Willy were as like their sires as peas, but she kept all her favour for the two little maids in their nurseries. One of these was called Rose the Red, and her mother, who loved her dearly, always dressed her in gowns of red. The other was called White Lily, and went ever in gowns of no colour. But neither of these small maidens in the least resembled their lady mothers.

They had eyes like black beads and voices like peacocks, and when they trod behind their grandam, from solar to kitchen, a castle in Barnesdale echoed to a sound like thunder in the hills.

'THE lady favours it,' said Much.

'She would,' growled Little John.

They were discussing their master's intention of venturing himself again into Nottingham town. The countryside seemed to have quietened down, and the Sheriff of Nottingham had proclaimed a shooting match to be held in the market square of his town on Midsummer Day. The prize offered was a silver arrow, with feathers and tip of pure gold, and all the best archers in the north of England were coming to compete for it. Nottingham would be gayer than she had been for many a year. Some people even held that the King would be present at the show, though others said that he was preparing to turn north against the Scots again.

Robin Hood said to his men, as he sat at supper with Maid Marian by his side:

'I think we must bring home that arrow to our lady.'

'Another trip to Nottingham town?' questioned Will Scarlet, pursing his lips.

'This time I will go with strength,' said Robin. 'And anyway, last time it was not the Sheriff laid hands on me, but the Town Guard, incited by an ill-disposed monk. The Sheriff was loath enough to keep me prisoner, and strove, as you know, to pass me on to the King's Grace for sentence.'

'It might,' considered Marian, 'be almost a good thing if he did catch you again, now that the King is in these parts. For our comely King loves a good archer, and having seen you win the silver arrow in his sight, he could hardly condemn you to death forthwith. Then you, meeting him man to man, could declare your loyalty to him, and I could beg your pardon, like a loving woman. So you could be no longer an outlaw, and we could be wedded.'

'Amen! But there are too many "coulds" in this story for my peace of mind,' intoned Friar Tuck, who had prescribed for himself since Maid Marian's arrival a dignity and gravity that were costing him sore.

'And when I am your master's dame, good Friar,' concluded Marian, 'you shall be chaplain at one of my southern castles.'

'*Gramerci*, gracious dame,' said the Friar faintly. He had no heart for more supper, and spent the rest of the evening murmuring in tones of horror to any one he could stop: 'Chaplain in a dame's castle! In the finicking south! It would kill poor Tuck. Robin must not go to the shooting in Nottingham town.'

Nevertheless, Robin went, attended by seven score strapping young men dressed in Lincoln green. They entered the town from the north-west, at Chapel Bar, and marched directly on the Market Place, a short distance and all through that quarter of the town that loved Robin Hood's name. The streets were thronged by folk in clean aprons and cloaks, with well-scrubbed faces, and when they saw the light-stepping archers stride past with chins up, and eyes looking neither to right nor to left, they winked and hastened after them. But when they reached the Market Place, the green archers dispersed amongst the crowd, and only five stayed with Robin Hood.

The Market Square was already packed, although it was the largest in England, being five and a half acres in area. In that side of it behind which rose the castle, was a high erection draped in red cloth and protected by a canopy. This contained the chairs of those lordly ones whose eyes must not be vexed by the midday sun. The King was not present. He had gone north to engage the Scots. But the Sheriff and his ugly daughter, surrounded by many town worthies, occupied some of the best seats, and in boxes on either side of them were knights and ladies from neighbouring castles, who had brought with them their children, waiting - women, squires, pages, and hounds. Tier upon tier of seats for spectators of lesser degree ran round two other sides of the square, and lest Midsummer Day should prove wet, they had been shaded by an awning. Much said to Gilbert of the White Hand:

'Mind, there's a plaguey striped red-and-white canvas fluttering down near the butts in a slight westerly gale. But this market is built on an incline. I reckon they cancel each other.'

Gilbert, whose eyes had been scanning the boxes, merely answered: 'The Sheriff has some ill-favoured fat mares in's stable to-day. Would you like a sapphire brooch to give to our lady?'

The fields around were bright with coloured tents, pitched by those of the competitors who had come from afar and been unable to obtain lodgings in the town. The number of men with five-foot bows on their backs, waiting at the end of the square left open, augured a long day's entertainment. All the free seats had been occupied since dawn, and from those set aside for schoolchildren arose a chirping, as from an aviary. All windows overlooking the scene had been draped with bright hangings, and were filled with comfortable family groups finishing breakfast. Below, hawkers of drinks, sweetmeats, and pies passed from stand to stand, crying their wares.

The green archers had arrived in good time. Two officers of the Town Guard were just stepping the hundred yards between the marksman's stand and the butts. The mob cheered them as they returned to bow in front of the Sheriff, in token that they found the field fair and true.

The target, which was called the clout, was made of wheat-straw, three or four inches thick, and faced with cloth, painted with rings of black, red, and white. The exact centre of its innermost circle, which was painted gold, was the pin-hole, into which young archers dreamt at night that they sent three arrows, each shivering the other. The clout was sloped backwards, and around it, on the ground, at distances of eighteen inches, three, six, and nine feet, other rings had been painted on the cobbles.

At length, looking mayhap bolder than he felt, the marker, whose duty it was to stand by the side of the butts signalling hits and misses, stepped to his post. In the silence that fell suddenly somebody could be heard explaining to a deaf aunt that the target, the centre, and the arrow that hits the centre are each known as the clout.

The shooting began, but Robin Hood, after watching the first few arrows winged, stood with his eyes fixed on the ground. He knew already that his band could shoot as well as any here at so easy a mark. The contests Maid Marian had arranged for them every day recently had been far more difficult, and they were in perfect trim after so much practice. He knew, too, that with so many competitors, hours must pass before the sport became interesting.

Hours passed, and all the usual things happened. A child that had been sitting with the strong sun on the back of its neck, swooned, and was carried from the scene. Two men who had drunk too much ale started a fight in the free seats, and were arrested and haled to the stocks. All of the choristers of St. Mary's Church stood up in their seats to watch this, and the people behind them shouted that unless their choirmaster forced them to sit again, they would demand their money back.   The day grew hotter and hotter, and although the arrow leaving the bow and sometimes finding the target sounded regularly, people began to drowse.   Then a nervous archer shot the marker in the ankle, and every one took fresh interest for five minutes, in case it should happen again, but were disappointed.   Presently the Sheriff retired to the back of his booth to take refreshment, the hawkers of food and drink did a brisk trade, and afternoon calm settled on the scene, because people with pies in their mouths cannot shout clearly.

It was during this half-hour that Robin Hood and his men shot for the first time, and folk who had been settling for a doze sat bolt upright, and began to nudge one another.   When the Sheriff returned to his seat, he was told that the green archers looked like to win the prize. 'Green!' said he, turning green himself.   He leant forwards, and peered into the ranks of the competitors at the far end of the square.   But already the six green-clad men had retired to wait their next turn.   All that he saw was a party of young fellows from Doncaster, who ought never to have entered for the silver arrow, but had hoped that on the day they might shoot better than they had been doing lately.

By the time that there were long, cool shadows lying across the square, the contest was being fought out between four bands.   There was a party of smart fellows from York City, one of whom must have been a wonder five years past. There was a party that had come all the way from South Wales. One of them had told Much that he thought nothing of this sport, for his uncle had once shot an arrow through an oak door, four inches thick, and the head had stood out a hand's breath on the inner side. There was a band from the Scottish borders — English side, they were careful to explain, though their speech didn't sound like it—and the green archers. Every one else was out of the contest, which had now been increased in difficulty, winners of a former round not being allowed to count hits into the rings on the ground. Blacks and reds on the clout itself were to be lost for further successes.

The party from Sherwood were left to fight out the finish with the York band. One of them, forgetting that a frayed bowstring may mean a broken bow, hurried to disaster. Yet their score, when they had done, was a proud one. Robin Hood put Gilbert of the White Hand forward to shoot first for Sherwood. Gilbert was not his best man, but nothing upset him, and the crowd was noisy now. Gilbert, as usual, did his best, taking up his stand, nocking, drawing, holding, and loosing as calmly and carefully as if he were alone with the clout in the forest. Will Scarlet, who followed him, raised hand-clappings and shouts of 'A keen loose!' and 'Bravo, green jacket!' Much came next, and gave place to Beardall, looking annoyed with himself, for after a wooden loose, he got a white. The old soldier Beardall, in spite of all Robin's teaching, still would draw his arrow to the ear, as if length of flight were his object. While Little John was shooting gracefully and steadily as ever, but tending, as ever, to bring his face to his hand, rather than his hand

to his face, the Sheriff turned in his seat and gave an
order to some behind him. Robin stepped forward, last
of his band, with the duty of finding the pin-hole if they
were to win.

He took his time, slipping up and down on his left
forearm the leathern bracer that helped the arrow to
glide smartly off the string, and saved doublet and
forearm. He put on and off the finger-tips of his right
hand a tab he had used often enough to know its feel.
At last he planted his feet firmly and took an arrow from
his quiver with his right hand, and laid it above the string
and across the bow. He pressed the nock home steadily,
laid his fingers to his bowstring, and bent forwards slightly.
Then, bracing the muscles about the small of his back,
and turning his head towards the clout, he began to raise
and draw his arrow, truly beneath the line of sight of his
aiming eye. He tightened his grasp on his bow, held
for the space of a butterfly's kiss, and loosed his arrow.
There was a sound of a distant plop, followed by a wild
yell. He had found the pin-hole. When he had done
this with his two other shots, people stood on their seats
and waved their hats. Amongst the cheering the word
'Robin' could distinctly be heard.

The silver arrow was his, but he was not done yet.
A giant figure shouldered through the guards around
the butts, and planted in front of the target a slender
white stick. It was a peeled wand of willow. Little
John nipped away, and hardly had he done so than Robin
Hood shivered the new target, so pale and thin that it
could scarcely be seen by some of the beholders. He
sped a second shaft to displace his first, and a third that
sent the wand in two pieces to the cobbles. Then he
went up to the Sheriff's box to receive his prize.

The Sheriff stood up in his seat, and leaning over his timber balcony hung with scarlet cloth, said in a disturbed, hurrying voice:

'I present the good arrow to the best worthy archer.'

Robin bowed as courteously as one king to another. In the same moment the cheers of the crowd were drowned by a great blast of horns.

'Woe worth thee, proud Sheriff,' cried Robin, seizing his prize from the Sheriff's shaking hand and darting back. 'Thou art ill to know!' And he drew his long bow to his ear again, but this time not in sport.

There was a dire fight that evening in Nottingham Market Place. Many arrows were winged, and several townsfolk had to be carried home with broken ribs, for when the Sheriff's men began to shoot at the green archers there was a panic amongst the spectators in the free seats. No women were slain, although many had their kirtles torn, and one female child fell out of a window. But when the green archers had fought their way to Chapel Bar, several of the Sheriff's men, with arrows sticking in them, were left lying upon the cobbles of the Market Place.

Robin Hood was the last of his band to quit the square. As he flew down a passage, so narrow that its walls on either side were worn shiny, he crashed into a limping man. Little John had paused in a doorway to draw an arrow out of his kneecap. He opened his brown eyes as he flung the bolt from him, and saw Robin Hood.

'Give me your dagger in my heart, captain,' said he, offering his broad breast, 'for I can run no further.'

'Not for all the gold in Merry England!' said Robin.

Much's face peered round the corner. He said:

'Hurry, master!' He saw what had happened, and added: 'Ay, 'twould be Little John we have to carry!'

Robin and Much, between them, bore the giant into the fields. By a well they laid him down, and all had a drink. Then Robin bowed his back, and Much, who could do no more, bundled Little John, who had now fainted, on to his master's shoulders. Robin shortly after fell into a ditch, and groaned for the first time.

'Don't stir, captain,' said Much. He pointed, and Robin saw that beyond this ditch lay another, and above that a hill covered by trees, on the top of which rose a square tower.

'Yon keep is one of those you helped Sir Richard at the Lee win back,' said Much. 'Now let him help you.'

He stumbled away, looking for a path, and returned ten minutes later, followed by half a dozen eager men-at-arms and Sir Richard himself. They came in good time, for the Sheriff's men were searching the woods with ban-dogs.

'Welcome be thou, Robin Hood,' said Sir Richard at the Lee. 'And Little John too! Come! Up once more, and then we will drop the portcullis and hale heavenwards the drawbridge. And, by Saint Quentin, no man shall disturb me while I play host to Robin Hood.'

Robin Hood brought the silver arrow to Maid Marian, saying: 'Here it is, lady.'

'*Gramerci!*' said she. 'I knew that you would win it. But I have heard that it was bait for a trap, Robin!'

She laid aside the fine linen that she was tearing into strips outside her lodge. The trees around were hung with bandages, fresh-washed, and slings, and jerkins and hose with rents in them. Maid Marian had, as every great lady should have, good knowledge of surgery. She had with her own hands anointed and bound up every broken head and limb brought home from Nottingham on Midsummer's night.

'That Sheriff is a false man,' said she, turning the silver arrow in her hands to mark the sunshine playing on its feathers of gold. 'And you did not see the King to get your pardon. . . . Welladay, the year is yet young, and I would ever sooner have a bold love than a lucky one.' She laid the arrow aside and gave her hands to Robin, saying: 'Shall we move into Barnesdale awhile after this affair?'

'No,' said he, 'we must wait here a little, lest any harm come to Sir Richard at the Lee. But I would sooner you sought a convent. I have a cousin, a nun in Kirklees Abbey . . .'

But Maid Marian refused to leave Sherwood, and a fortnight later the band was completed by the arrival of Little John, well in his body but still walking halt. He reported that the Sheriff had ceased to besiege Sir Richard's castle near Nottingham, partly because he had no hope of gaining it, except by starvation, and partly because the knight had sent a quelling answer to his demand for entry. Sir Richard had dispatched a herald to the Sheriff, telling him that he held all his castles and lands directly of the King, and to the King alone was answerable for what guests he harboured. The Sheriff had forthwith ridden north to find the King, who was himself besieging the castle of Berwick to no purpose.

The Sheriff was absent many weeks of high summer, and during them the outlaws, all healed of their wounds, and happy in so brave a captain and lady, took what they pleased in Sherwood and on every road around. The forest was filling with fair young calves. Hind and hart had got their rich summer coats. The stags had grown their new antlers, and were laying on fat. Much brought down a buck at five hundred feet, and Robin Hood a Hart-Royal. They never had better sport.

On an August morning, when there was a heavy dew in the long grass of the orchards belonging to the abbeys of the greenwood, and the apples were yellowing, Robin Hood went forth with Maid Marian to try a new bow. It was of yew that had been seasoned for three years before it had been made into a bow. After that Robin had kept it in store another two years. Five winters and five summers, said he, were needed to bring the perfect bow to maturity.

'And the perfect wedding?' asked Maid Marian.

'Do you tire of the Sire-wood, lady?' said Robin, halting on the height to which they had attained, and looking down on to Birkland and Bilhaugh. Range upon range of tree-tops lay below them, pale blue at this early hour as waves of the sea. The day promised to be another of great heat, and the lower skies were rosy.

'I would live in the Sire-wood all my life,' said Maid Marian. 'As well you know. Winter and summer,' said she.

'Well, praise God, it is not winter yet,' said Robin through set teeth.

They descended hand in hand towards a group of silver birches inclining towards a green ride.

'Nor,' said Maid Marian presently, 'are ladies yet afraid to venture alone into your kingdom, as you see.'

A solitary figure, mounted on a black palfrey, was toiling through the bracken towards the ride. This lady had evidently travelled far and lost her way. Her fine red gown was torn and wet, and her small face, inside its coif, was wan and wild. When she caught sight of two green-clad foresters, she seemed for a moment inclined to fly. But her palfrey did not answer to her spur. Robin put back his hood, and ran towards her, crying:

'God save you, lady! What can I do for you?'

She looked at him with mournful black eyes, and said faintly: 'Oh! If you are an outlaw, lead me to Robin Hood.'

'Our Lady has led you to him, dame,' said Robin, dropping on his knee.

She gave him her thin hand, and said: 'God save thee, Robin Hood, and thy fair page. For the love of Our Lady, grant me a boon.'

'Gladly,' said Robin, 'but first you must know that this page you salute is Maid Marian, Queen of the Greenwood.'

'I am the unhappy wife of Sir Richard at the Lee,' said the strange lady, turning to Maid Marian. 'Yesterday my eyes were as bright as yours, for I went hawking with my gentle knight by our riverside below our castle near Nottingham. But even as I let my tercel gentle fly, men-at-arms set upon my lord, and bore him to the ground. There were many of them, and we had gone forth attended by but two pages and our young children. Sir Richard has been carried, shamefully bound, hand and foot, to prison in Nottingham town.'

Robin Hood slung his new bow behind his back, and pulled forward his horn.

'What man has done this deed?' he asked.

'The proud Sheriff,' said she, 'for love of Robin Hood.'

'Comfort you, dame.' said Robin. 'Your lord shall clasp you again. As for this Sheriff, I see I have been patient too long.'

Thunder rolled in the distance as he blew his horn, and the party that set out for Nottingham castle an hour later had to shelter at the forest edge before entering the shining wet town.

'We shall need dry bow-strings to-day,' smiled Robin Hood to his men.

Maid Marian led Sir Richard's dame to her forest lodge, and there offered her a seemly feast. But although the dame had eaten nothing since yesterday's dusk, she would not take a morsel to recreate herself. She said:

'Alack! fair damsel, tease me not with your courtesy. I cannot eat while my wedded lord lies in bodily danger.'

'Robin Hood has said that he will bring your gentle knight back to you, madam,' said Maid Marian.

'Oh! I know he will do his best,' said the dame, wringing her hands.

'I think that if I were Sir Richard at the Lee, I should grieve to know that my dame fasted,' said Maid Marian.

But the dame was obdurate, so Marian called Annet to bring her child. When the dame saw Robin a Dale, her tears flowed, and she said:

'I have seven children, who shall be fatherless.'

Maid Marian had a gloomy afternoon, for what time her guest was not weeping, the heavens were streaming forth hail and lightning, and thunder clattered around, advancing and retreating like a cautious enemy.

Towards evening the storm drew to a distance, and some mocking sunshine began to dapple the glittering glades, and the sound of branches drip-dripping was overcome by faint notes of a bugle-horn. Sir Richard's dame dropped on her knees, and began to tell her beads. Maid Marian clapped her hands to order a banquet.

The victors were glad to see what a feast she had commanded for their home-coming, for they were all wet and weary men. As Sir Richard clasped his trembling dame to his breast, Robin said aside to his lady: 'Madam, the Sheriff is gone.' And he jerked a thumb downwards at the damp sward.

'I reckoned it must be so,' said Maid Marian. 'Where did you get him?'

'In the Houndsgate,' said Robin. 'The right place. Oh!—and through the heart with the first arrow from my new bow.'

THAT autumn the King of England was defeated rather by pestilence and famine than by his enemies. With the spring he sent his favourite, young Hugo Despenser, to make a thirteen years' truce with the Scots, and prepared to enjoy himself hunting in his northern chases.

In the Inglewood, which stretched sixteen miles from Carlisle to Penrith, he found amazingly few deer. He called up the chief forest officer of Plumpton Park, and asked the man how many bucks the late King had slain here in a single day's hunting. The man, falling on his knees, whispered: 'Sire—two hundred.' The King gave him a mailed gauntlet in the teeth.

Robin Hood had spent Christmas on the west coast this year, and passing through Cumberland on his road to Uttersdale, where Maid Marian was wintering in Sir Richard at the Lee's castle.

The King proceeded to make a royal progress through Lancashire. When the south-east wind blew shrewdly in these parts, folk said 'twas a Robin Hood wind. Once when the royal transport broke down, and the King had to mount a mule or stay where he was for a night of frost, a groom who did not recognize him said:

'Ay, sir, you've got Robin Hood's choice now.'

'And what choice is that?' asked the King.

'Marry,' answered the man, slapping the mule's quarters, 'this or nothing.'

The King mounted, gnawing his lip. He heard within the next few weeks of Robin Hood's pennyworth —lightly come and lightly gone, of Robin Hood's yard —five feet or the length of a long bow, and of 'going

round Robin Hood's barn,' which meant reaching the
right conclusion by the most roundabout way. On an
August evening he saw above him, on a wild moor, a dark
castle, rising nobly against skies the colour of a ripe apple.
He asked to whom this castle belonged, and was told:

He saw above him, on a wild moor, a dark castle . . .

'Sir Richard at the Lee, who sheltered the murderers of
the Sheriff of Nottingham last year, a crime that has
never been avenged.'   He rose in his stirrups, and ordered
some of his large attendance: 'Ride up to that keep,
demand entry in the King's name, and when you have
won in, take all there prisoner. So will I do to every
castle of that traitor knight.'

Sir Richard at the Lee came heavily to Sherwood to tell
Robin Hood that he was once more a landless man. He
had only escaped death by flight, and he had brought
with him his wife and all his daughters. What was worse,
winter would be here again in a couple of months, and
this year he would have no castle in which to shelter his
own womenkind, let alone Robin Hood's lady.

See page 202

The Sheriff stood up in his seat . . . and said . . . 'I present the
good arrow to the best worthy archer'

Maid Marian received this blow of fate with a proud bearing. She said:

'With the spring I will come again. When the deer draw to the dales from the moors, look for me too. . . . Meanwhile, I consent to hide me in a convent. But I will not go to any in the north, for I think that this King might have me out. I will wend south to my own country of East Anglia, to the great priory founded by my grandsire. And I will take with me Sir Richard's womenkind at my own cost, for I owe them thanks beyond all cost.'

And indeed, though she had spent twelve weeks of hard weather enclosed amongst them in Uttersdale, not a soul of Sir Richard's family yet knew her by any other name than Maid Marian.

Maid Marian sent Much and Gilbert, disguised in false beards, into York, and there they sold for her to rich merchants a collar of diamonds, and got for her instead three horse litters called *charettes*, suitable for carrying ladies of rank on Ermine Street. Robin Hood lent his love noble horses and stout grooms to attend her on her passage south, and her setting out on an October morning was a noble sight. The *charettes* had curtains of rose-scarlet leather lined with flame silk, and inside, abundance of white velvet cushions and furs and Turkey cloths. Gilbert had bargained like a Jew with the York merchants, and in the end they had thrown in with the furnishings of the litters two strange small beasts that came out of the mysterious East. Marmosets, they were called. Much thought that they might serve to amuse the ladies and children on their tedious journey. The coats of the horses had been polished till they shone like satin, and all the outlaws acting as grooms had trimmed their heads neat and round as nuts.   There was wreathing early mist pierced by silvery sunshine, and the procession looked as if it must be bound for fairyland.

Sir Richard's dame rained tears as she parted from her careworn husband, leaving him an outlaw amongst outlaws.   She clung round his neck and bewailed her piteously.   Maid Marian, with her red-gold locks all braided out of sight under a stiff coif of gauze, sat upright and serene as the statue of a holy saint above an altar. Her lips, which were like a thread of scarlet, smiled steadfastly upon the company drawn up to witness her passing.   She bowed repeatedly from side to side as her *charette* began to move and waved her handkerchief a long time.   Her last words to Robin, as he bent over her hand, were:

'With the spring I will come again!'

The King sat in council in a great stone chamber of his castle at Nottingham.   On his right hand sat the elder Despenser, newly created Earl of Winchester, on his left young Hugo Despenser.   The grim barons and knights on either side adown the long oaken table looked sourly at the King's smooth favourites.   The King himself looked melancholy.   It was eleven months since he had left London, and he was tired of the cold and comfortless north, where he had very nearly been taken prisoner by the Scots.   Although from his earliest days he had been bred to be a warrior, he had no inclination for the life of hardship.   He was wishing, this slaty grey afternoon, that he was warm in some little room of his palace at Westminster, where there would be tapestries, figured with lozenges of gold, on the walls, and Genoese fiddlers making a jolly noise, and a handful of cushions to tuck behind one's long spine as one shook the dice-box.

He was as handsome a man as any in his realm, six feet high, broad-shouldered and straight-limbed. He had inherited the regular features, clear grey eyes, and curling golden hair of his dead mother, a princess of Castile. When his high-nosed, terrifying old sire had died too, he had thought that now he should be happy. But his father had been in his grave seventeen years, and still Edward of Carnarvon had to do things he disliked. Nottingham, of course, was far more comfortable than most of the places in which he had been forced to dwell lately. Some attempt had been made to hide the masonry of this gaunt hall. It was hung with canvas cloths, on which figures, heavily outlined and coloured with splodges of angry red and brown, were engaged in some pursuit, probably bloodthirsty.

The King took a green grape from a silver-gilt platter at his elbow, and listened to the tedious men around him. He had a right to be furious, for he had spent a fortnight at his royal lodge of Clipstone in Sherwood Forest without the least satisfaction. The season for hunting the hind and the doe had just opened, and he had scarcely seen a beast worth following. This council had been summoned to discuss the state of his northern forests, the depredations of outlaws therein, and the measures to be taken to check such abuses. But when he had said that Robin Hood must be captured and his band dispersed, every one had pulled long faces and begun to make difficulties, just as they had done when he had insisted on bringing the crafty Bishop of Hereford to trial for high treason.

They pointed out now that Sherwood was five-and-twenty miles long and ten miles wide, and the men inside it knew it much better than those outside. Ever since the murder of the Sheriff of Nottingham, attempts

One of the 'King's Deer' in the forest of Sherwood

to catch Robin Hood had never been relaxed. A serious number of highly trained soldiers and verderers had never returned from these expeditions. Some of them were suspected of having joined the outlaws. The knight who had sheltered the Sheriff's murderers had been declared a traitor, and all his castles and lands had been seized in the King's name. He had simply gone to live on the King's venison in the Sire-wood with Robin Hood.

The King swore by the Trinity that he would not be so trifled with. 'I will issue a proclamation,' he said, 'promising that whoever brings me the head of Sir Richard at the Lee shall inherit all that knight's lands.'

An old baron, with a gnarled brown face and deep-sunk eyes, sitting at the foot of the table and coughing villainously, cleared his throat to say that he was afraid this would hardly do.

'Because,' he explained in his broad native accent, 'the only fellows who will try for such a reward, sire, will be men with nothing to lose—pure rascals. And even should such an one succeed in carrying off the knight from the very arms of Robin Hood, he would never be able to hold the lands Your Grace proposes to bestow upon him.'

Another northerner sitting opposite, Sir Goodwin Hawtaine by name, agreed with this, and added warningly: 'Give the lands of Sir Richard at the Lee, sire, to no man you wish well.'

The Young Despenser whispered sneeringly behind his hand to the King that both these gentlemen owned property marching with that of Sir Richard at the Lee.

'One would think,' said the King, rising suddenly, 'that you all wished Robin Hood well.'

The council dispersed, and the King strolled over to a window, with his right arm flung round the shoulders of his olive-skinned young favourite.

'They don't wish Robin Hood well, sire. I think,' said Hugo Despenser in rapid French, 'they must, at heart, be ashamed of such outlawry in their country. But so long as the outlaws keep to the King's land and only take the King's deer, and perhaps some moneys from fat bishops and abbots—well, well . . .'

He looked out of the window in front of them, with interest.

'What are you looking at out there?' said the King. 'You know there is nothing cheerful to be seen.'

He yawned, and went off to the stables to play chuck farthing with some grooms there. Down in the stables he was happy, seated on plenty of sweet-smelling straw, with a flagon of ale at his elbow and hounds snuffing his hose. The scene, lit by torchlight, was all gold, and every face around the King was merry. Presently a man in the livery of a verderer edged up to him and said:

'If you would see good Robin Hood, sir, you must do as I say. You must use cunning.'

A PROCESSION of holy men had left the village of
Hucknall-Torkard and was wending its way north
through the forest of Sherwood. The November morning was sharp after a night of frost. Overhead the sky
was a rejoicing blue, and underfoot fallen leaves were
frozen on to little pools which spat at meeting boots and
hooves. The foremost rider of the party overtopped
all his companions. He wore the dress of an Abbot of
the Cistercian Order—a great white cloak, hiding his
figure from throat to knee, stiff riding boots, and above
his cowl a broad-brimmed hat of white felt, secured by
tasselled cords. He alone rode a horse, a magnificent
brown charger, with saddle and housings of purple
leather and silk, and a gilt bridle. A man in the habit
of a groom walked by his side, leading a delicate white
greyhound. They were followed by five white-clad
monks on pattering mules, and a couple more grooms,
leading sumpter horses on whose backs were large baskets
with leathern coverings.

A cock pheasant that had been roosting in the lower
branches of a tree, flew into the forest, uttering a squawk-
ing cry, and every one started and looked after it. The
Abbot passed a red-gloved hand across his mouth, and
forced a laugh. He bent to ask his groom:

'Are we drawing near the place?'

The man answered: 'One of his places, sir. He is
no fox that hath but one hole. The haunt to which I am
leading you is known to us verderers as his stable. But
if we fail to find any trace of him there, I can take you on
to his well, and his larder.'

'Do so,' said the Abbot, and began to hum a French song, a lament for a warrior called Monsieur Simoun, who had fallen in arms against his King.   His monks took up the refrain, and although its words were not holy, yet the effect of their chanting was solemn.   If they had wanted to advertise their coming to the outlaws of Sherwood, they could hardly have found a better way.

So they proceeded into the depths of the forest, and a pair of legs, wriggling in the higher branches of an oak overhanging their path, disappeared, and there was a swishing sound as a man ran away through dry bracken. But as he wore tunic and hose of the same colour as his surroundings, no one could follow his flight far.   The groom leading the greyhound, which had begun to tremble, looked at the Abbot.

'Good,' said the Abbot.   'The flying hare warns the deer.'   And he motioned his men on.

A little later they saw several figures flickering around a thicket of scarlet-berried thorn, but when they came abreast of the spot, only the scent of wood-smoke and a few charred sticks told them of a stamped-out fire. They passed on into a part of the greenwood where most of the trees were limes, and the track grew narrow and more miry.   The greyhound gave a yelp, and the Abbot's horse shied, as a tall, russet-clad man, with a bow on his back, leapt into their path.

He took the brown charger by its gilded bridle, and said with a good accent: 'Sir Abbot, by your leave, you must abide here awhile.'

'Who are ye?' asked the Abbot loudly, turning in his saddle to perceive many more bronze archers appearing from behind the trees on either side to close in around his monks and grooms.

The man answered, pushing back his hood and disclosing a red head: 'We are yeomen of the forest, who live by taking our King's deer.' He stared a second at the Abbot's groom, who had caught his master's eye and had nodded silently. Then he went on gaily: 'You have churches and garths that bring you rich rents, my lord. Give us poor outlaws somewhat for charity.'

The Abbot looked the outlaw in the face, and said in an odd, bitter way: 'I am a rich man, you think? Ha! Let me tell you that you are wrong. After a fortnight spent in Nottingham, where your King now abides, I have escaped with only forty pounds in my bags. One must, you know, make friends of the barons around His Grace, if one is to gain an audience.'

He turned in his saddle again, and ordered the grooms leading the sumpters:

'Unload, and give these gentlemen all the King has left your Abbot. Indeed His Grace is a dear master. Well, I had almost sooner my money was shared amongst the robbers of his forest than those of his council chamber.'

An enormous archer, who had spread his cloak on the ground, and was watching two others counting the forty pounds into it, straightened his back to cry in threatening tones:

'Be merry as you will about the King's lords, Abbot, but keep your tongue from his name.'

The Abbot plucked his white cowl about a face in which two pale eyes glittered.

'What,' said he, 'do the yeomen of his forest love the name of Edward Carnarvon? This is not the fashion in London, nor any of his great cities. Have you not all heard how we have a King who would sooner spend his days hunting the fallow deer than sitting in his council chamber?'

Somebody shouted: 'Small blame to him,' and several people laughed.

'Indeed his tastes are strange for royal blood,' proceeded the Abbot musingly. 'He will dice all night, and have to borrow from his grooms at dawn to pay his debts. Is that not so, fellow?'

The groom leading the white greyhound said: 'Yes, my lord. He has had coin off me.'

'Keep your mouth shut about it then,' cried one outlaw, and 'Cheer up,' advised another.

'Alas! he abaseth his dignity by preferring the society of servants to that of his equals,' said the Abbot, and his voice sounded as if he would weep.

'Why,' asked the red-headed outlaw at his bridle, 'what equals has the King?'

The Abbot sounded pensive. 'None, I have heard— at such deeds as digging a trench, or thatching a house, or hammering a breastplate. He can also sing a merry catch, ply a lusty oar, and ride a good race . . .'

'You need say no more,' said the chief outlaw. 'We are all King's men here. Robin Hood is my name. Thank you for your charity, sir, and I hope we may meet again. For though you are an ill subject, you are a brisk payer.'

'I thank you for your courtesy,' said the Abbot, fumbling inside his cloak. 'And if your name is Robin Hood, receive from my hands a letter sent to you by your King.' He produced a roll of parchment, tied around with yellow silk from which dangled a broad red seal. On one side the seal bore the likeness of a king enthroned in his royal robes; on the other a king fully armed, mounted on a galloping horse, with his shield held up to his chin and his right arm brandishing a sword.

Robin Hood knelt to receive the document, and pressed its fair seal to his lips.

'If you cannot read,' continued the Abbot blandly, raising his voice, 'know then that Edward his King greets Robin Hood well, and bids every yeoman of his forest come into Nottingham town to break bread at his table.'

The outlaws drew close to watch their captain unroll and read the King's letter. Some looked suspicious and muttered that no priest ever brought such good news. Others said that they had known their comely King would never condemn them unheard.

Robin Hood ran a bright eye over the letter, rolled the crackling parchment up, and buttoned it inside his tunic. He said with a great sigh and his hand on his heart:

'Welcome, right welcome. . . . I think I have never seen so brave a letter. For seven long years I have desired to see my King's face. . . .' He cast off old memories, seized the Abbot's bridle again, and cried suddenly in tearing spirits: 'Sir Abbot, you must dine with me to-day under my trystell tree.'

He set his horn to his lips and blew a single long blast.

'By St. Austin!' said the Abbot, as answering cries came from every quarter of the fading woods around them, 'Robin Hood's men are more at his bidding than the King's.'

Robin Hood led the Abbot and his monks a mile and more into Sherwood, and brought them to a forest lodge of timber, where a banquet was being set. Clear fires were roaring up towards the blue heavens, and serving-men were setting, upon a single long table, platters and cups of silver-gilt, garnished with jewels, and flagons of blood-red wine and nut-brown ale, and trenchers of bread, white as a lady's hand.

'By St. Austin,' swore the Abbot again, 'I dined once with the King in his stone lodge at Clipstone, and got not such fare. When His Grace railed at the stale bread, old fish, and pale-faced pasties, he was told that it is not easy to bring a fresh banquet so far into his forest.'

'I am sorry to hear it,' said Robin Hood, 'for we are less than a league from Clipstone here.'

'Even so,' said the Abbot, dismounting and looking around him curiously. 'Your men have a quick brave look,' said he, 'and you have too some goodly hounds and horses, I see. The King, for all his faults, knows a horse when he sees one. He has spent, I am told, more money than he should, buying up the famous stud of Earl Warenne at Ditchling in Sussex, and more time than he should in those stables. He boasts that his Welsh harriers can discover a hare sleeping. . . . It is a great pity.'

'What, of all this, is cause for pity, sir Abbot?' asked Robin Hood shortly.

'That he was born a King,' said the Abbot, sounding again as if he must weep.

Robin Hood blew three short notes on his horn, and two dozen of the men commended by the Abbot for their quick brave look stepped forwards to face their captain and his guest. They fiddled with their bow-strings as if waiting for an order.

The effect on the Abbot was ghastly. He covered his face with an arm, turned stumbling in his long skirts, and shouted in the French tongue: '*A moi!*'

Robin Hood caught him by the sleeve.

'Sir Abbot! Sir Abbot! Be of good cheer. My men mean no harm. I had thought, while we wait our food, that it might please you to watch some shooting.'

The Abbot, though the larger man, was easily stayed.

'Some shooting?' he repeated faintly. His features, which were noble and regular, had gone chalk white, and his pale eyes showed bright with anger and fear under his shadowy cowl and broad-brimmed hat.

'At a goodly mark,' explained Robin Hood.

'A goodly mark,' said the Abbot, drawing himself up with a long shudder. His wild gaze, searching the swaying glades, fell upon two white poles garlanded with flowers, which a couple of men were sinking into holes in the sward.

With an effort he recovered himself, and said in measured tones: 'Ah! the last rose garland of the year, I see. But your marks are set full fifty paces too far apart.'

Robin Hood smiled as he answered: 'Every man that fails to shoot through the garland loses his tackle, and shall further receive a buffet from the next fellow that succeeds. Will this make for good sport, do you think, my Lord Abbot?'

He stepped away to shoot first himself, and soon from beneath either pole sent an arrow singing through the garland hanging on the top of the other.

The Abbot, standing in his great riding boots with legs astraddle, slapped a thigh in most unpriestly manner. He tilted his broad-brimmed white hat back from his brows, and whistled with surprise and pleasure. Gilbert, who followed his master, shot no worse. Next came Little John and Will Scarlet. But Little John was not himself to-day. Every time his loose was at fault—either wooden or dull. He failed even to hit the poles. Will got once through the garland. So Gilbert buffeted Will, and Robin Hood pursued Little John with raised fist. The Abbot cheered them on, and swore by St. Austin

that had the King such archers he would be sitting in
Edinburgh instead of Nottingham now.

At last only Gilbert and Robin were left in the contest,
and they each shot another round to decide which should
be victor.   Robin held his last arrow too long, and it
missed the garland by three fingers, so Gilbert started to
rush for him, bawling:

'Master! Your bow's mine. Stand fast and take
your pay.'

'I shall deliver my good tackle to my good guest,' said
Robin, offering his bow to the Abbot.   'And I think I
would sooner take my buffet from him.'

'Would you?' cried the Abbot.   He rolled up his
white gown from a muscular forearm, cried 'Hola!' and
gave the prince of outlaws such a blow that he all but
felled him to the ground.

'Thou art a stalwart priest!' cried Robin, staggering.
'I trow there is pith in that arm.   Canst shoot as well?'

'As well as Edward of Carnarvon,' answered the Abbot,
flinging away his hat, and putting back his white cowl
from a comely head of long fair curls.   He stretched out
his right hand towards Robin, who had dropped on one
knee, and said softly: 'Yes, I am your King.'

The citizens of Nottingham could scarcely believe their
eyes when they saw their King come riding into their
town, clad in Lincoln green, with Robin Hood by his
side, and behind them five of the King's knights also in
forester's dress, mounted on mules, and escorted by two
hundred outlaws.   They guessed that Robin Hood and
his men had taken the King prisoner, and that they were
marching on the castle.   There was a panic at the North-
gate, and fat merchants and marketing wives knocked

the breath out of one another, hurrying for shelter. When they got to their houses they bolted their doors and shuttered their windows, and waited for the trouble to begin.

The King laughed heartily when he saw Nottingham Market Place cleared of all but truant children, questing hounds, and a few old crones bent double with rheumatism, helping themselves along on sticks. 'The hinds bark alarm,' said he to Robin Hood. He called out to one of these ancient gossips that she need have no fear. 'Robin and his King are friends now.' She shook her crutch at him, and answered in a high, cracked voice: 'Bless your sweet face, I never thought otherwise. I run because I have poor neighbours count on me for their news.'

The glad tidings spread quickly, and the streets became as full as they had been empty. During the fortnight that followed, the little plaster and timber taverns crouched up against the castle rock did the briskest trade in men's memory. For they got the latest rumours. Just above them the King was feasting Robin Hood every evening, and that good knight Sir Richard of the Lee, to whom His Grace had restored all his castles and lands. The King was reported in merry mood, because he had done in one day what his officers had striven in vain for many years to achieve. With a royal smile and a few noble words he had won the outlaws of Sherwood to be his for ever. When great men meet they know each other's minds swiftly. The story of the King's disguise and bold adventure into the forest won him more popularity than all his pompous progresses of the past six months.

The King's stay in Nottingham drew towards its end, and the Queen arrived from York bound for London.

On a late November day Robin Hood summoned all his men to meet him outside the castle. He asked them how many of them would go south with him to serve the King. Eighty-seven handsome fellows stepped forward. Most of them were young bachelors. The Queen rode out of the castle on a hawking expedition as they mustered. Her name was Dame Isabeau, and she richly deserved her name, for she was a most beautiful lady. Her skin was the colour of ivory, and her eyes were as soft and dark as black velvet. She wore her ebony hair packed away inside a coif of gold gauze and gems, and a jacket of white brocade trimmed with ermine skins, and sea-blue skirts sewn with fleur-de-lys of silver. She rode a milk-white palfrey, and carried a hawk on her wrist.

When she saw so many handsome young men, her black eyes swelled, and she beckoned Robin Hood and said to him in her broken English: 'Will all these men serve the King?'

Robin knelt and answered her: 'Ay, and well, I hope, madame.'

'Stand up,' said she. 'I cannot hear you.'

Robin stood, and she looked him up and down right freely.

'So you are Robin Hood, the prince of outlaws,' she said. 'Do you know, I think I am somewhat of an outlaw myself.'

Robin, with his eyes fixed on the castle battlements, answered gravely: 'All great ladies are, I have heard, madame.'

She smiled without mirth, said: 'I hope you will like London,' and, giving her palfrey a sharp cut with her riding rod, passed on.

Much went that evening to search for his captain

The Abbot, standing in his great riding boots with legs astraddle . . .

inside the castle. He felt a yokel amongst so many smart pages, and ladies in gowns full of silk, and finicking squires and great lords. He had not volunteered for London and the King. The truth was, that he had for some time past been courting the widow that dwelt near his uncle, the carpenter, at Sneinton. Much's father had died and, very unexpectedly, left him his mill. Now that Much was an outlaw no more, and the owner of a mill, the widow had accepted him.

He found Robin Hood, looking unfamiliar in a long scarlet gown that swore with his hair, leaning in a window and looking out at dark skies and tossing tree-tops. Robin heard him out, then answered, poking a finger at the topmost button on Much's best tunic:

'I understand very well, old sobersides, better than you think. You see,' running his finger up and down twenty buttons and making a whirring sound, 'I am hoping to have a wedding myself now.' He added: 'My lady is a ward of our King, you see.'

Much went glossy pink, and stammered that he hoped the sweet lady was in good health.

'I hope so too,' said Robin.

Much was present to see Robin Hood and his eighty-seven men, all attired in the King's livery, pass out of the Bridlesmithgate a week later. He cheered loud as any. But he could not catch his master's eye, because his own eyes were awash with tears.

Next day he was married to the cooper's widow, and they set out together for their mill, the bride seated upon a pillion behind the bridegroom, and clasping him tight round the waist. Much rode his dapple-grey colt, and his favourite hound Tomson capered alongside, barking foully. They were very merry.

MUCH settled down happily in his mill. It was on the borders of the forest, so although he never took a deer or even a bird nowadays, and always slept in a bed within four walls, he did not feel too strange. His wife proved to have a much sharper tongue than he had expected, and whenever he went into Nottingham she went with him, so he got no chance of lounging in taverns and hearing how the world was wagging. He soon lost touch with most of his old friends, but was so busy with his mill that he scarcely missed them. Presently he began to wonder if many of them would recognize him if they happened to meet him in church, say, or boating on the river with his wife and child. For Much, who had been large as a bachelor and outlaw, now that he was a married man and a miller, had waxed enormous.

Friar Tuck was his only link left with his old life. Regularly at Easter, two mountainous figures might be seen, gravely fishing, side by side on the banks of the Idle. Much's wife did not favour the fat Friar, so Much kept his guest out of doors as many hours as possible, a scheme that suited all.

Two New Years had passed since Robin Hood had gone south to be the King's man, and Much had neither heard nor seen anything of him since. Even Tuck, who was always on the move, had failed to meet any one from London who knew more than the name of the prince of outlaws. Many did not even know that. His arrival in the capital with his eighty-seven gay archers had been a nine days' wonder.

Friar Tuck and Much sat angling together at dusk of a

moist spring day.   There were cowslips and a couple
of hounds on the bank beside them, and what was more

*Friar Tuck and Much sat angling together at dusk of a moist
spring day*

to the point, a flagon of ale and a basket of cold pasties
and cheeses.   Much's wife had been too weary to cook
a hot supper to-day, for Much's son was cutting his teeth
and had kept all in the mill awake last night.   She had
begged her husband, that if he and his old companion must

come in after dark, they would take off their shoes and refrain from song. As things happened, they were not feeling like song this evening, for either the spring or the river damp had got into their bones.

Much lifted his black felt hat to scratch his head, and said to Friar Tuck: 'You didn't hear any sound—like as 'twas from the forest—just now?'

The Friar turned on his stool, his face round and solemn as the rising moon, and answered: 'Not I. But I have heard that there are folk in the forest again o' nights.'

'Folk,' echoed Much. 'What sort of folk do you mean?'

'Our sort,' said the Friar. He corrected himself. 'The sinful sort we once were. But there! if you've heard nought, 'tis surely gaffers' talk.'

'I go into the forest so seldom, and never after dusk,' said Much, glancing towards it. 'That's the law. But are you telling me that men we once knew are back in yonder?'

'So I have heard,' said the Friar. 'Men who went south—with him—and couldn't abear it.'

'There it is again,' said Much, interrupting him.

He clutched the Friar's sleeve, and as they listened, straining their ears in the thin blue darkness, both thought they heard the note of a bugle, but so far, faint, and wavering that neither could swear to it.

'Some lad trying his first horn,' suggested Much uncertainly.

'Law or no law,' said Friar Tuck, gathering his skirts, 'I am going to see that lad.'

The two heavy men left their rods and baskets lying, and hurried towards the line of trees rising solemn against the eastern skies. They were not in fettle, and made slow going. It was Much's hound Tomson that found the strangers—three shabby fellows crouched amongst the bracken in a glade magical with spring buds and moonshine. One of them was bending over another who was lying on his face as if exhausted. The third, rising to a giant height as he spied figures advancing towards them, drew from his belt something which glittered in the moonlight. But Much's hound, instead of barking at them, had begun to run round them, snuffing and uttering excited cries.

'By Cock and Pie,' swore Friar Tuck, ''tis Little John. Friend, friend, put away that knife. Here's Tuck and Much bursting blithe to see you. And whom else of the old band have you here?'

'The captain,' whispered Will Scarlet, rising from his knees.

Friar Tuck scuttled forwards and pommelled the prone figure, crying: 'Robin! Sweet Robin! Look up! Here's your chaplain, heard you calling him. What ails you, captain?'

He was answered by a feeble 'Holloa!' and Robin Hood struggled to his feet and stood swaying. He was thin as a hermit. He spoke as a man that speaks in his sleep.

'Did you know,' he asked them, 'that in London no birds sing—and a man cannot sleep? I did not sleep or eat for seven days or nights before I went to the King to ask his leave to visit the seemly chapel I once built in Barnesdale. His Grace has given me seven day's leave—seven days . . .'

'You are kindly welcome, captain,' said Much awkwardly.

'Nay, but you do not know me yet,' said Robin, shaking his head. 'I have no money left, and of all my merry men, but two.'

'Four now,' said Much stoutly. He asked in an aside of Will Scarlet: 'The lady has stayed in the south, belike?'

Little John gave a warning growl, but Robin Hood had heard the question, and the thought of Maid Marian seemed to work a change in him. With a sudden effort he raised his horn to his lips, planted his feet apart, and began to blow again. The music grew, raising ghostly echoes in the moonlit glade, and to the surprise and joy of all, ghostly men began to answer it. Dressed in rags, wild of hair and eye, they were hardly to be recognized as the gay archers who had marched out of Nottingham to serve the King. When they saw who had come back to them they went nigh mad with joy. Some flung themselves on the grass to embrace his knees, others turned somersaults, several wept openly.

Robin Hood put away his horn and flung his arms wide.

'Welcome! welcome! my wight young men. I am come once more to shoot at the dun deer with you, and I think I shall never leave you again.'

Down in the mill that night, Much's wife, rocking her fretful babe, heard the sound of horns in the forest. She ticked her tongue in her teeth, and said to the four walls of her bedchamber:

'I hope that doesn't mean we are to have that sort of thing beginning again!'

Her hopes were vain. Robin Hood never went back to London and King Edward. He stayed in Sherwood and Barnesdale, an outlaw once more. Gradually a band, as skilled and as large as any he had ever commanded, gathered around him. He seemed as merry as ever. But those of his men who had known him in the old days said that he was changed. His sorrows while he had served fair false King Edward in the south had nearly slain him. He never alluded to them, but when the news of the King's deposition reached Sherwood, he did not seem surprised. It was followed, within ten months, by rumours that the King had been secretly and horribly slain. Many folk did not at first credit this, but Robin at once gave orders for masses to be sung for the soul of Edward of Carnarvon.

Queen Isabeau had found a most brutal outlaw to love her, Roger Mortimer, a wild Welsh marcher baron. Together they misruled England in the name of her young son, Edward of Windsor, who was but fifteen. Their rapacity and cruelty were so great that within three years all men believed them guilty of the late King's death. They came to Nottingham to hold a Parliament, bringing the young King with them. They held him in such thraldom that no man might gain access to him, and all entrances to the castle were guarded by Welsh mercenaries.

But on a misty autumn night a small band of mailed men entered the castle by means of a secret passage in its rock. In the yard of the castle they met a young knight in armour, with an unsheathed sword, who said: 'Follow me.' He led them upstairs, and they seized Dame Isabeau's love, although she cried in the French tongue: 'Fair son! Have pity on gentle Mortimer.' The Queen's favourite suffered a traitor's death, and she was carried to a fast castle in the south, where she was kept in captivity until the day of her death, but honourably attended, because she was the King's mother.

The young King proved as mighty a warrior as his grandsire. He went to the borders to fight the Scots and overseas to fight the French. But his glorious victories cost England dear, and his people groaned beneath his taxation. When he came on progresses they fled his face, lest his officers should seize their goods.

On a fine spring morning early in the new King's reign, Much said to his wife: 'Busk you in your best, for we are bidden to a wedding to-day.' She said: 'Whom that we know would be wedded in May? All maidens hold it a most unchancy month.' 'But this bride,' said Much, 'is a lady of a high courage.'

So they put on their best clothes and rode into the greenwood, and saw a right fair lady called Maid Marian wedded to Much's old captain. The bride brought with her no red gold but that which sprayed on her shoulders under a chaplet of woodland flowers. She had given all her fortune to the young King for his wars. In exchange he had granted her leave, either to stay in the convent where she had been living for two years past, or wed where she pleased. Robin Hood, who had refused for seven years to wed her, because she was a great heiress and he was an outlaw, and had been refused her by the late King while he served him honourably, took her most joyfully now that she had not a penny.

They had a perfect May Day for their wedding, with a light blue sky full of puffy clouds, and just enough breeze to blow the scent of hawthorn and the cries of lambs and thrushes about the forest. Little John gave away the bride, Will Scarlet was groomsman, and Friar Tuck performed the ceremony. Sir Richard at the Lee was present, and brought with him his lady and his four youngest children. His two elder daughters had married brave young knights some time ago, and his son was at the wars with the King.

After the wedding there was an archery contest and single-stick play and wrestling and a great banquet. They danced and sang on the night of Robin Hood's wedding until the skies began to grow pale for dawn, and some country folk who were there said that there were strange guests helping the music. They swore that they saw, couched amongst the drifts of bluebells or flying hand-linked in the moonshine around the great trees, little people, no higher than your knee, whose laughter was like running water. The gentlemen amongst them wore green hoods and rode upon grey-hounds, and the ladies all had green kirtles. There were also damsels of less than human size, with little heart-shaped faces and green hair hanging to their heels, who peered from tree-trunks and waved their hands. Others, garlanded with forget-me-nots and lilies and carrying pipes of reeds, crept up from the water-meadows with the dusk mist. One fellow was positive he saw a milk-white unicorn wearing a collar of gold, dancing with a lion-cub in the forest that night. But with daylight all these strange guests vanished, or else the village people, straggling home through the sun-shafted coppices, with crumpled gowns and nodding heads, were too much mazed with sleep and warmth to notice them any more.

Robin Hood and Maid Marian took no harm of having been wedded in May. They lived together happily in Sherwood and Barnesdale for two-and-twenty years to the certain knowledge of many.

During these years there was a new Sheriff in Notting-ham, an easy weakling fellow. Robin took to going into the town when he pleased, and once, disguised as a potter, sold his wares so cheap that he won the heart of the Sheriff's wife, and she asked him to dinner. After he had feasted with her, he sent her his last two pots by the hand of a little urchin, with Robin Hood's humble duty.

This Sheriff rode for his life on the only occasion that he ever met Robin face to face. For there came to Nottingham a boastful knight called Sir Guy of Gisborne, who said that if ever Robin and he met, the world should know which was the better man. He was high of heart, for he had slain two of Robin's best men in Barnesdale and taken Little John prisoner. He told the Sheriff to look well to Little John, and went off into the forest, wearing a horse's hide over his armour, a disguise that gave him an awful look. The Sheriff waited as he had been bidden, at the forest's edge, with Little John tied to a tree and closely guarded, and presently to his relief he saw a knight wearing a horse's hide returning towards him. The knight flung a battered head on the sward and asked as his reward for slaying Robin Hood that he should now be allowed to hang Little John. The Sheriff said he thought that little enough to ask, and the knight unloosed Little John from the tree. But when the giant outlaw was free, the knight put a bow in his hand and himself pulled forward a bow from under the grim hide which he wore. The Sheriff's men cried: 'Robin Hood has slain Sir Guy!' and took to their heels. Their master, having a horse, got home first.

Two-and-twenty years after the wedding of Robin Hood and Maid Marian a great pestilence came to England out of the East. It was called the Black Death, and it carried off a third of the people of England. Three Archbishops of Canterbury died of it within a twelve-month, and even a child of the King, a most beloved little damsel, called Joan of the Tower. People fled from town to town in hopes of escaping it, but it outstripped them. The harvests rotted in the fields for lack of reapers, there was murrain amongst cattle, and whole villages were left without a single inhabitant. Families were swept away so that no heirs could be found for rich manors. In priories and abbeys whole communities, from superior to novice, perished.

After the pestilence had departed, new people came to the silent villages, and when their children said to them: 'Who is Robin Hood?' many of them could give no answer, or would say: 'You had better ask the gaffer down at the forge. He was here before . . .' Others, who had kept their ears open, said: 'Why, he was a great outlaw of these parts, and did the poor much good. In many houses of these parts, when we came, there was a faded green garment and a cap and an ancient bow hanging hid up in a corner cupboard. . . . But Robin Hood must be dead years past.'

The children did not like to say that they had seen him, and that although he had frosty curls and walked helping himself along on the shoulder of an enormous old man with a white beard (like St. Joseph on the wall-painting in the village church) he was still the finest archer in the world. To amuse them, he had made them hang daisy-chains from branches of trees in the forest, and he had shot through the flowers, neater than any young archer they had ever seen.

But the children were not allowed by their parents to wander in the Sire-wood, so they said nothing. And when they grew up, many of the boys amongst them did not want to be famous archers like Robin Hood. They wanted to be master gunners. For with the gun, which

was the new weapon of war, you could batter your enemies'
castles to pieces.   Quite often, as yet, the gun did not
behave as it should, and the men working it got killed.
But it was undoubtedly far more exciting than the old
long bow.

Nevertheless, the old long bow continued to win
battles for many a year.   It was still winning them more
than six score years later, when a Kentishman who had
learnt the art of printing overseas set up the first English
printing-press at Westminster.

He was kept very busy, for every one who could afford
such a thing, and many who could not, wanted to possess
a printed book.   Also noble ladies and gentlemen with
time on their hands, arrived continually at his house,
asking if they might be shown printed books in the
making.

A certain young knight of East Anglia arrived on a
May afternoon to see the master printer.   He was
already in debt, but he was wooing a court lady and was
of a hopeful disposition, fully aware that he was a handsome and taking fellow.   The master printer, who was
a grave, white-bearded man, wearing a black velvet cap
with ear-flaps and a long sage-green gown, said to his
fashionable guest:

'I am sorry that you have come on May Day, Sir John,
for I have let my prentices run to the May Games this
dawn, and not all of them are yet back.'

However, he led Sir John into his workshop on the
ground floor, and showed him some goodly books: *The
Sayings of the Philosophers* and *The History of Jason*.
Sir John showed most interest in a book telling you how
to play chess.   He said, looking out of the window at the

townsfolk in their best clothes, streaming back into London from the green fields where they had been gathering spring flowers and dancing and mumming all morning:

'You know, Master Caxton, you ought to print a book of the merry gestes of Robin Hood.'

The master printer considered, and answered: 'I have never seen a book of Robin Hood.'

'Oh, neither have I,' said the knight, 'but every soul in England loves the jolly outlaw, and keeps this day as his festival. I have myself kept in my household for seven seasons past, a very rascally, lazy knave who is good for nothing but acting Robin Hood in Maytime.'

The master printer beckoned up his chief assistant, a clever young foreigner called Jan van Wynkyn, from Worth in Alsace, and asked him: 'Wynkyn, have you ever seen a book of the deeds of Robin Hood?'

The Alsatian answered, bowing elegantly: 'Nevare, sare. But we 'ave in my country, too, such a legendary figure. Our peasants call 'im *Robin du Bois*.'

'Be careful, Wynkyn,' said the master printer solemnly. 'In England you must not doubt the name of Robin Hood.'

'But,' protested Wynkyn, spreading out his hands, 'in England you yourselves say of a tall story: "'Tis a tale of Robin 'Ood."' He stepped back to his desk, saying decisively: ''E nevare live!'

'Robin Hood a tall story!' said Sir John Paston, going pink to the roots of his yellow curly hair. 'By the Mass, master prentice, you will be doubting King Arthur's knights or St. George's dragon next.' And he left the building after buying the *Book of Chess*.

In the workshop the discussion continued.

A nice-looking young prentice called Copland said to Wynkyn shyly: 'You know, Master Jan, I think you must be wrong in saying that Robin never lived. For once when we were in Yorkshire, my brother Bob and I saw his grave.'

A blackavised, sharp-featured fellow, whose forearms were stained with ink, dumped a parcel of paper at Copland's elbow and said with a grin: 'That's right, Bill. Robin Hood lived and died, so he must have needed a grave. But he happens to have been a Ludlow man, like me. An arrow he shot into the roof of Ludlow Church is still to be seen in our Fletchers' chancel there.'

From the back of the room, a bronzed, bearded man, who was at work with wood blocks and a hammer, ceased work to ask in a deep bass voice: 'What was he doing in Wales, when every one knows he was a Zummerset man?'

'Somerset,' interrupted a little skipping bald fellow, who was cleaning type with a pin, in the full light of the windows. 'He certainly came from Matlock. Robin Hood's Tor was our Sunday afternoon walk when I was a child.'

The most industrious prentice in the workshop, who was picking letters out of a box with a pair of pincers, said without raising his head: 'Haud your noise a'! Robin Hood was a Scot!'

This raised such an uproar that Wynkyn had to leap on a bench and explain that he was sorry he had never known before that Robin Hood had been so great a traveller as well as so great an outlaw.

As he drew off his hose that night up in the prentices'

dormitory, Wynkyn said to Copland: 'I think many people in England would buy a printed book of Robin Hood.'

'Why,' said Copland, 'I think so too. But the master is old. And there is no written word of Robin Hood— only many songs and old wives' tales transmitted from tongue to tongue. One would have to go up to Nottingham and Yorkshire, where he certainly lived and died.'

'How did he die?' asked Wynkyn.

The young prentice began to babble enthusiastically:

'Why, when he was old and vexed with fever, he went for surgery to an abbey of which his aunt's daughter was Abbess. She was a greedy woman, in league with an ill knight called Sir Roger of Doncaster, and they believed Robin rich. So she opened a vein in poor Robin's arm, and they locked him in a high chamber of the abbey, and left him there to die succourless. But our brave outlaw, with some of his last strength, blew three faint notes on his doughty bugle-horn, and Little John, who was waiting anxiously outside, rushed in, breaking bolt and bar. When he saw what the Abbess had done, he asked his master's leave to burn Kirklees nunnery to the ground. But Robin, noble to the end, said that never in his life had he hurt a woman, and he knew that all he needed now was a grave. So Little John raised the wasted form of Robin Hood in his great arms, and Robin drew his trusty long bow for the last time, and shot an arrow out of the window, and where it fell there was he buried. I have seen the pretty place.'

'Humph!' said Wynkyn, getting into bed and drawing his coverlet up to his nose. 'That would make a sad ending for a book.'

'It is a very noble ending,' said Copland indignantly,

'and no sadder than the death of Arthur, which every one buys.'

'Well,' said Wynkyn, blowing out their light, 'if it is true, I suppose one would have to put it in.   But very shortly.'

'Some people think,' said Copland's voice, beginning to sound drowsy, 'that Robin still sleeps in the greenwood in England, and that, like Arthur, when his country has need of him, he will come again.'

'*Charmant!*' said the Alsatian.   'When I am a master printer, I shall certainly print a Robin Hood.'

'So shall I,' said Copland, suddenly wide awake again.